Horses Dream of Money

Horses Dream of Money

stories

Angela Buck

TUSCALOOSA

FC2 is an imprint of The University of Alabama Press

Inquiries about reproducing material from this work should be addressed to the University of Alabama Press

Book Design: Publications Unit, Department of English, Illinois State University; Director: Steve Halle, Production Assistansts: Phil Spotswood and Bryanna Tidmarsh, Production Interns: Katelyn Kern and Laura Kimlinger
Cover image: A Horse in Armor, artist unknown, German, ca. 1560–1570; digital image courtesy of the Open Content Program, J. Paul Getty Museum
Cover Design: Lou Robinson
Typeface: Adobe Caslon Pro

"Coffin-Testament" adapts language from Sir Thomas Browne's *Hydriotaphia, Urne-Burial.*

Library of Congress Cataloging-in-Publication Data is available from the Library of Congress.

ISBN: 978-1-57366-188-1
E-ISBN: 978-1-57366-890-3

For Ervin Buck, 1924–2020, and Sue Buck, 1927–2020

TABLE OF CONTENTS

The special skill of each individual machine-operator, who has now been deprived of all significance, vanishes as an infinitesimal quantity in the face of the science, the gigantic natural forces, and the mass of the social labor embodied in the system of machinery, which, together with these three forces, constitutes the power of the "master".

—Marx, *Capital Volume 1*

I desired liberty; for liberty I gasped; for liberty I uttered a prayer; it seemed scattered on the wind then faintly blowing. I abandoned it and framed a humbler supplication; for change, stimulus: that petition, too, seemed swept off into vague space: "Then," I cried, half desperate, "grant me at least a new servitude!"

—Charlotte Brontë, *Jane Eyre*

Work

THE SOUND OF THE MACHINERY IS TERRIBLE TO ME. It meets my life with a life of its own, which in its unreality has a reality more real than mine, one that I am more willing to believe in because it never breaks down and never doubts itself. But it also consoles me in its own way, carries me through the day, even though I am grown and old enough to console myself.

I sit on a high-backed stool when I am tired, but usually I stand while I do the work that must be done, and done well. There is an air of quiet conviviality in the place, and I mostly enjoy the jocular hiccups that erupt all around me while I work fastidiously and with an unrelenting devotion to my work. The foreman can see this in me, can see that I work hard and with great zeal, and although I have not been rewarded for this work, he lets me know in his way, by never looking at me and never saying anything to me, that I am the best and also his favorite.

Sometimes I look out the window and see a bird and cry out to anyone who will listen, although inwardly, and usually these people are dead or living far away or imagined. Sometimes I place my hand on the shoulder of the person to the side of me, in my mind only, and leave it there for several minutes.

It is terrible to think of all of this actually happening, my filthy shoes, my shirt full of holes, plugging fake diamonds into the plastic monkeys that pass before my eyes. There is a whistle in the air, and I am whistling it. Another monkey. Now and again I am struck by the quiet dignity of these animals. When there is only one person in the world whom you care for, and that person is a monkey, and he is fake, that is a great pity.

Now I will turn my attention away from these monkeys. I am building in my mind a great ship. At the sight of this ship I become calm. A great sense of well-being fills my entire body, and it is terrible to not understand what is happening when this is happening to me. I return again and again to this ship of my own making and wonder if it is real or not. Now I will take myself down to the harbor and labor there while I am laboring here.

The sailors here look like friendly monkeys, like the ones I am making at work, but here they are real and work for me. These sailors are like my children, like bodies of children emptied of childhood and filled with a sea that does not age. Sometimes I watch them from above while they work and am filled with the mystery of their ship-making.

The sole contact I crave is moving all around me in these men, in the ships they are building, and in the sea. Now and then my family passes by, and my youngest brother allows his balloon to float up to the sky where it hovers for several minutes before floating out to sea. I am often moved by my own visions and do not question the reality of what I see before me. My own mother emerges from the cabin of the ship to tell me about the dream of this ship, but I know it is only a story.

Now many kinds of birds and animals gather at the base of the ship. They bite my mother, and she bleeds, but I will not help her. All of these things look more pleasant than they are in reality. I allow them to occupy themselves with whatever it is that they are doing, the sailors and also the birds and my brother and also my mother, until, all at once, I can see that they can see that I am looking at them. We all look away. We all return to our work.

THE BALLOON-MEN

SORRY, I COULDN'T HEAR YOU.

Were you asleep?

No, not asleep. I was just thinking about something.

Tell me about it.

I've already told you so many times.

This time might be different.

It won't be different. It's always the same.

Remember what we talked about?

How nothing is ever the same?

And nothing is ever nothing.

It was the silence that woke me up. It startled me actually. It was a Wednesday, but it sounded like a Sunday. Even quieter than that. I went to the window. No cars. I looked down into the street. I saw a pair of legs flopped on the sidewalk, the head and torso in the shadows. That didn't alarm me because bums always sleep there. They stay up all night drinking and sleep during the day. What scared me were the birds, the rock doves that usually hang out on the streetlights. Three of them scattered in the street, dead, their multi-colored breasts, purple and green, still vibrant.

I took a shower after that. Habits, I guess. The drops of water on the enamel seemed loud compared to the silence in the street. When I came out of the shower I looked into the office. My husband was up late doing work and slept on the office couch the night before. He wasn't there. I wanted to ask him about the birds in the street and the silence but he was already gone. I didn't hear him leave. He just left quickly, that's all. He didn't make coffee. That's why I didn't hear the grinder. He didn't want to wake me up. And he was cutting back on caffeine. He drank green tea and stayed in his socks until the second before he left; then he slipped into his shoes. And closed the door so quietly that I didn't hear it. He didn't lock up. That's how thorough he was. He didn't want the sound of the lock to wake me up. I checked the front door. It wasn't locked. This confirmed my hypothesis. I hadn't been sleeping well. He didn't want to interrupt my sleep. That was plausible, a plausible tale.

I dressed. I put on something nice, grey pants and a blazer. I wore a thin, red scarf. It was the end of winter, almost spring. I normally would wear heels with that outfit, but I didn't that day. Not very practical. For walking or running. Running from something. I might have to get away. I put on boots instead. They looked OK—not great, but good enough.

I made coffee, put half of it in a thermos for later, and ate my usual breakfast: two eggs and a piece of toast with butter and jam. By then it was six o'clock, and I had to hurry to catch the bus. Luckily I packed a lunch the night before. I put that and the thermos in a leather bag with my other work things and left.

The bus stop was close to my apartment. I could get there in less than five minutes. I would try to get there early because the bus at that hour always came early. At first I thought I had missed it. There was no one at the stop. Normally I caught the bus with two other regulars: a black man dressed in a chef's uniform and a nurse. Actually I don't know if she was a nurse. She just looked like one, the kind of woman you could imagine taking your blood pressure. Kind in a way, but also indifferent to suffering, because she saw it every day. She had that kind of face. Maybe she wasn't a nurse. Maybe she answered phones or sat in front of a computer all day. It's possible those jobs produce the same kind of face. Then I realized the bus couldn't have come already. I knew because it left tracks. It disturbed the gravel next to the curb, left a high ridge of pebbles. This clue never failed me. So I waited.

I waited for a long time. The chef didn't come, the nurse didn't come, the bus didn't come. There were no cars actually, no birds, no people, just silence, and me dressed for work, holding my bag upright with my feet, and the strap in between my hands, like I always did on every other day.

There used to be an Arby's across the street, but it closed two years ago, and no one else bought it. I went to look at my-self in the window. I wanted to see another person. I wanted to reassure myself. Everything looked normal. I was dressed for work. I laughed because my face looked so serious, almost grim. There were sharp lines in between my eyebrows, and my mouth was pulled into a straight line. Relax, I said aloud, imitating my husband's voice. There's got to be an explanation for this. Then I turned and ran back to the bus stop. Anyone could have stolen my bag, I thought. There are so many desperate people in this town. And desperate people will do anything.

I decided to walk. It was only a mile downtown. I was glad I wore the boots instead of the heels. I looked for movement in the houses, in the apartments. It's still early, I thought. People are sleeping. And in the spring there are marathons and parades. That's why they close this street. It happens all the time—I just didn't notice before. And it's nice in a way, the peace and quiet. Normally that street was loud: motorcycles and bums smashing bottles. I tried to enjoy it for once.

By the time I reached the office my feet hurt. Even the boots weren't very practical. No shoes were really when you considered the realities of survival. I wished I had worn my tennis shoes or hiking boots. I pulled at the outer door but it was locked. Usually the janitorial staff left it open for me. They must have forgotten. I walked to the side entrance. On that side was a courtyard with three benches, empty of course. They always were at that hour. The side entrance was also locked. I rummaged through my bag looking for my keycard. I never used it because, as I said, the janitors usually left one of the doors open for me.

I heard something move behind me. I didn't look but I could hear a rustling sound, like a flag flapping in the wind, but softly, barely a ripple. I looked furiously for my keycard. Did I even bring it? I was so distracted in the morning.

I saw a shadow move over the surface of the glass, from left to right, and growing in size as it moved. Still the rustling sound, like razor-thin metal crumpling in someone's hand. The shadow was in the shape of a man.

I felt the plastic keycard in my palm. It was my third sweep through the bag. How it evaded my grasp the first two times I do not know. Maybe it felt my panic and wanted to tease me. I felt the edge of the laminate peeled away at the corner. With shaking fingers I waved it in front of the keypad. The door un-bolted. I felt something brush against the back of my head. The shadow crossed my face.

Inside I could look. I was safe enough to look. It wasn't a man, not exactly. It was a giant man-shaped helium balloon floating in the courtyard, left over from someone's extravagant birthday party or bar mitzvah. It drifted along the side of the building, tapping the glass as it went.

I was in the large glass atrium with square concrete plant-ers filled with palm trees and an elevator at one end. I almost never came in that way. No one came in that way, except for clients. So I wasn't alarmed when I found it empty. I took the elevator up to the twelfth floor and went to my office. I sat in my office for a long time with my head on the desk. I was tired from the walk and my feet hurt. My boss usually didn't come in until nine. I could take a nap. I half-slept and half-thought about my boss asking me to fill in a big hole with sand. He handed me a shovel. At first I couldn't find any sand. Then when I found some it was too far way. Somehow I brought the hole closer. I can't remember how this was accomplished. But then the blade of the shovel broke in two.

I heard a tapping at the window. My blinds were drawn. They were dusty. I sneezed. I tried to ignore the tapping, but it grew louder. I pulled the blinds up, but slowly, because I didn't want to see. I had already seen enough. I was tired of seeing.

It was the giant man-shaped helium balloon. His wide face was inches away from my own. He had floated up twelve stories and was outside my window. Naturally, because that's what balloons do. They don't have any agency. They float because their insides are lighter than air. There's nothing strange about this. It's a matter of science.

Now I could see his face clearly. He had a fifties style haircut, pomaded into shape, and big blue eyes that looked sideways. And a smirk. He looked exactly like one of those old Bob's Big Boy statues. Except he wasn't holding a hamburger.

And that's when the balloon spoke to you?

No, that was later. You're jumping ahead. Right then I said something to it. I said: What's happening? In a whisper. I said it to myself also, but I thought he might know. I thought you had stopped listening.

No, I've just heard that part before. I was letting you talk.

I appreciate that. It's kind of you. It was then that I admitted to myself that something had gone wrong; something catastrophic had occurred. The world died, part of it, or maybe it was me. There had been a break. I was worried about its finality. I hadn't seen another person all morning.

Except for the bum's legs, in the shadows.

That's right. I thought about that. I remembered his legs. I wanted to be near them, near something human, anything human. I felt desperate. The balloon-man continued to tap against the glass. Harder and harder, with tremendous force. It's amazing what air can do. It seems so soft. But he had a tornado inside of him, or a hurricane, some unstoppable natural force. The glass starred and crumpled inward, like a boil about to burst. Then I ran—

But you didn't go home.

No, I didn't go home. I wanted to see my husband. I wanted to see if he was still alive. I knew it was impossible, but I had
to see. I had to at least check. He worked three blocks away
from me. Sometimes we would have lunch together at a deli
in between. I actually convinced myself that we would do that
today, that we would have lunch together like normal. When
I passed the deli I didn't even look at it. I just pretended it was
open and someone was setting chairs out on the patio. But of
course it was closed, and when I rounded the corner I saw the
balloons reflected in the window.

Balloons?

There were more of them now. Three or four. Some looked
like Big Boy, but there were women, too, with blonde hair and
big blue eyes looking sideways, looking crazy, and that same
smirk, like a kid's drawing, with the mouth off-center, tugged
to one side, crooked. They wore white aprons stained with
blood.

That's a lot of detail to remember.

It could have been cow's blood or pig's blood or even, I
guess, the blood of a chicken. Anyway, I didn't see it all then.
I saw it later. Right then as I was turning the corner I just saw
that there were more of them, that they had *multiplied*. And
their eyes, not round or oval but flat on the bottom and curved
at the top, like the windows of a cathedral, with the pupils
nailed to the lower right corners, all of them, looking sideways.
A feeling of absolute terror came over me. Have you ever felt
that? It's like walking around with no skin. You are completely
exposed. The balloons moved slowly and at the same time fast,
like clouds. They seemed to just float along, but actually they
were covering a lot of ground, and with an inalterable sense of

purpose: total determination. When I reached my husband's office the front door was unlocked—I was so relieved. I went in and locked it from the inside. I felt safer in there. It's a brick building, not glass like mine. I pushed a desk up against the double doors just to be extra safe. I went to my husband's office. I knew he wouldn't be in there. Why would Ben be in his office when everyone else in town was gone?

Everyone except you.

Everyone except me. And the bum I saw that morning. I told myself this is crazy. He's gone like everybody else. I told myself that, as I took a step toward his door. It was closed, but the light was on. I could see an orange glow through the frosted glass. I said: Ben's dead. Aloud, to prepare myself for the worst thing, for the inevitable.

But he wasn't dead.

You're jumping ahead. I knocked on the door, but of course nobody answered. I opened the door. The office was empty. See, I said. It's empty like everywhere. Ben hasn't been spared. Whatever's happened has happened to everyone. I felt almost satisfied. There was a logic to it, a consistency, something to order the madness. It helped me to make sense of it, to understand it, to—

When you say 'it,' what do you mean exactly?

I mean this madness that had taken hold. This evacuation, the feeling of having lost everything—things you didn't even know you could lose, everything you took for granted, like being evicted from the Earth.

I notice you're speaking in second person now.

I'm trying to relate my experience to another person, or maybe distance myself from it. I sat down at Ben's desk, looking at his things. I wanted something of his, something that smelled like him. But there were only work things: papers and his computer, paperclips and pens, nothing personal. I found a piece of paper with his handwriting: square and in all capitals. He had written: THIS GUY'S A JERK. And below that: EGGS, BREAD, COFFEE, CHOCOLATE FOR JULIE. Seeing my name in his handwriting made me feel safe. I folded up the piece of paper and put it in my pocket.

Then the phone rang.

Yes, yes. It did. Someone ripped off the top of my skull—

You're speaking metaphorically?

—and looked inside. It had been so quiet, and now this phone was ringing. A little green light lit up above the keypad. I didn't answer it right away. I thought it was the balloon-men, that if I answered it they would say terrible things to me, break me down psychologically, until I let them in willingly, almost welcomed them.

But it wasn't the balloon-men, was it?

No, it was something much worse. I picked up the phone. My hand was shaking so much that I had to cradle the receiver with my other palm. I heard a voice in mid-sentence say, "... galleys should be done by five. I'll email them to you, and you can tell me what you think, whether you like the design or not." It was Ben's voice. "Ben?" I said. "Julie?" he said. "What are you doing at Franklin's?" "I'm not. I'm at your desk." "What?" he said, laughing, and his laughter set me at ease, and at the same time made me feel crazy. I was in his office, wasn't I? "That's so weird," he said. "I was just talking to Devon about their brochures and the new logo. I guess I hit the other line. Are you at work? Or is this your cell phone?"

"Ben, is this a joke?" I shrieked. "Where are you?" Then he stopped laughing. "Julie, babe, what's going on? What's the matter? Are you crying? What's going on?" I told him everything that had happened that day: the silence, the dead birds, the bum's legs, the vacant city, the balloon-men, and now this: "I'm in your office, holding your phone, looking at a piece of scrap paper with your handwriting on it. It says: This guy's a jerk. And: eggs, bread, coffee, chocolate for Julie." Silence. I could hear fingertips on paper. "I just wrote that note. I have it right here. I was in a meeting with the insurance guy—" "Where am I, Ben? Where am I? Are you in the right world or am I?" He told me to stay calm. He said: "Go straight home." He said: "I'll be there." Then the line went dead. Yes, Ben was right. I should go straight home. And he would be there. And everything would be fine.

But things weren't fine, were they?

I wanted to believe it, but I didn't believe it at all. Wherever I was, Ben couldn't help me. Nobody could. If I ever got out alive it would be because I found a way out on my own. Nobody could help me.

Except for the bum.

Except for him. I told myself I was going home to see Ben, but really I was going home to see the bum, to see if his legs were still sticking out of the shadows, to see if anyone was alive in this world, if anything moved on my side, other than the balloon-men. That was my only hope of getting back to Ben's side, the right world, the normal world.

But you didn't think you would ever get back.

Not right then. Right then I had a pretty dim view of my prospects. Or I should say I felt like something very small and unimportant caught in a large and swift-moving current. There was a slight possibility that this small, insignificant speck of dust could make its will felt. It wasn't impossible, but it was not likely.

Now you're speaking of yourself as an object, a thing.

That's how I felt. It wasn't a sense of inferiority or anything like that. I could just see very clearly how totally fucked I was. That was a neutral observation, not a value judgment.

I have a hard time understanding that.

You can't think yourself into that position. You have to feel it. But then within the depths of that totally fucked feeling, you can actually see what's possible.

And that's where the bum came in.

Exactly. I don't really want to call him the bum anymore.

Give him a name then.

Ok, Tony. His name was Tony.

I found the keys to the company car in the office. There was a back stairwell that led to an underground garage. I left that way, found the car—it was a van actually—black with the company logo on the side in yellow. I had to hurry. I thought Tony wouldn't be there anymore. He would have woken up by now and was probably as clueless as I had been that morning. He was probably wandering around the city to see if anyone else was alive. And the balloon-men would be after him, too. I drove up the ramp. In the rectangle of blue at the top, I could see their feet dangling—they were waiting for me. They knew I would come that way. Their feet were cartoonish, the shoes crudely drawn—no laces just black half-spheres. Some of them had square gold buckles, like the kinds pilgrims wore.

It sounds like the shoes were important to you.

I'm trying to convey the terror I felt. They looked soft and puffy, but they weren't. I knew the slightest kick would send me flying off the road, crushed by a tree or the side of a building. And it would all be over.

Part of you wanted it to be over?

Yes, but I wasn't ready to die just yet. I thought there was a chance of getting back, the fact that Ben was still alive, that I had just woken up here—I thought it could all be undone.

Through effort?

No, not through effort. Through something like grace, but not the kind conferred by an intentional god. More like accidental grace, an indifferent god. I thought this was a mistake, a contingency, and another accident could undo it. I couldn't make that happen, but if I kept myself alive long enough it might happen to me. I crashed through the gate and made a sharp turn over the embankment. I could see them in the rearview mirror, two dozen of them now, crowding together like cannibals, like a pack of dogs, following me, not quickly, but at a slow, even pace—you would call it leisurely if not for the murderous look on their faces—never speeding up, never slowing down, but placid, confident in the knowledge they would get me eventually. They clearly took great satisfaction in torturing and killing, and that's why they took their time with it.

I drove through all the stoplights. This seems like a joke, but it's true: the balloon-men stopped at the red lights. They were law-abiding citizens. You never can tell, can you, who the real maniacs are? Anyway, that's commentary. The important thing is that it bought me some time. When I turned onto my street I began looking furiously for Tony. I couldn't believe it. He was still passed out in the empty alcove across from my apartment.

What did you think he would do for you?

I wasn't sure. The only thing I thought—and this wasn't even a thought but an instinct—was that I needed someone else in this world, anyone, it didn't matter who, the who part was meaningless, it could have been anyone. Once I parked the van though, and approached him, my old self came over me: who is this person? Is he dangerous? The phrase "total stranger" was on a loop in my head. And also I wanted to please him in a way. I'm embarrassed to admit that—

Anyone in your situation would.

Yes, that's true. But people have strange ideas about themselves. They think they are exceptional in some way. They don't understand how circumstance erodes all of our ideals. I couldn't see his face very well. The shadow didn't fall in the same place—it was later in the morning—and now it cut across his shoulders, just below the collarbones. I found his shoulder in the darkness. I gave it a shake. I said, "Excuse me sir, something terrible has happened."

"To you or to me?" he said. He was chewing something softly in his mouth, and after he said this he spit it onto the sidewalk. It was red and globular; spit bubbles formed at the edges.

"To both of us," I said. "Everyone in the city is gone except for us. There may be more, but—"

"That doesn't concern me."

I was kneeling next to him. My face must have been very close to his. I could smell his breath but I couldn't see him. "Aren't you worried?" I said. "Haven't they come for you, too?"

"No, they don't care about me. It's you they're after." He said this with total confidence, but it wasn't even confidence because it was so obvious, like saying what day it was, or your mother's maiden name. A fact, I guess.

I could hear the balloon-men coming for me. It was green lights all the way.

"Will you help me?" I said.

He said he would, but he wanted me to do something for him first.

Did you do it?

Yes, I was desperate. I was grateful for the darkness. I didn't want to see his face. He smelled faintly of urine. I undid the top of his pants. The button was broken and he was using a length of rope for a belt. I remembered something someone said once: if you tug at a knot it gets tighter. You have to work it softly, with your fingers. He wasn't wearing underwear. His penis was surprisingly clean. It tasted like soap. He was bigger than Ben, and harder, but he didn't take as long to come. I was grateful for that. I could hear the balloon-men coming. Now it was like the sound of wind through a metal tube. "They're coming," I said. "Don't stop," he said. He petted the back of my head. He said, "That's good. You're a good girl," and at the end he shuddered and called out the name of a girl—Desiree—probably an old girlfriend or maybe a prostitute. Are you judging me?

No, I'm not judging you.

His cum dried on the side of my face. It cracked when I talked. Does that disgust you?

Does it disgust you?

Yes.

But you were also turned on?

Only out of habit. Only my body found pleasure in it. It was mixed with disgust. That's what made it shameful. It wasn't a pure pleasure. It was work. Tony said, "You've done it. They've stopped." I looked. He was right. The balloon-men were stuck at the intersection before my apartment. The light had stalled. It was red, and they could not go. They looked furious. Tony laughed, and a hand came out of the darkness, the index finger extended. "Serves them right, those fuckers," he said. I said I was going home. He said, "Come back tomorrow. It's not over yet." I didn't care. I went up to my apartment. I made something to eat. I watched Tony's legs. He never moved. I wondered if he was a handsome man. Maybe tomorrow I would see his face. I still wanted to please him. I'm ashamed to admit it, but it's true. It's hard to take your side when something awful's happening to you and you're all alone. That's the recipe, the exact recipe for cruelty.

I think that's a good place to stop.

But I haven't finished my story. You can't leave me. When will I talk to you again?

I don't know.

THE DOLL

MY FATHER AND I ARE DRIVING ACROSS STATE LINES to buy an antique doll. We take his truck and drive on highways and backroads.

We don't see another driver the entire time. We pass a white house on the side of the highway where my mother lives with her new husband. It's fall, and everything's turning the same shade of brown.

When we reach the store, it's closed for the weekend, but we can see the doll in the window.

She's wearing a threadbare velveteen gown and a pair of high heels. Her breasts are protruding from beneath the fabric. Her eyes look both sad and excited.

I can see my father's reflection in the window. He's nearly pressing his face against the glass. He looks like a man in love.

"Well, we came all this way," he says and turns the rusty handle.

The door opens wide.

We head straight for the doll. My father reaches her first and very delicately lifts her up by the waist, looks at her for a second, and hands her to me.

"She looks a little bit like someone I used to know," he says. His voice is trembling. He leaves twenty dollars on the table.

On the way home, I hold the doll on my lap while my father drives. He keeps glancing in our direction.

"Are you going to give her a name?" he asks.

"No," I say.

When we return home, there's a message on the machine from the owner of the shop. He sounds frantic, in tears almost.

"How did he find us?" I ask.

"Men have their ways," my father says.

The owner says he'll drive all night.

"Have her ready," he says.

The doll is not concerned. She's been here before.

My father, on the other hand, is genuinely distraught.

I can hear gravel roll in the driveway.

My father and the doll are already gone.

A few days later, I get a letter in the mail. Inside is a picture of my father and the doll watching television in a motel room and a note that says:

I can't keep the happy women happy. I can only keep the sad ones from killing themselves. Love, Dad

BIRD DREAM

I CANNOT SAY FOR SURE WHAT HAPPENED.

The bird came through the window, and you caught it with both hands but not before dropping a wink to every man in the room.

And the window doesn't matter much, except that it may be the only thing that saw the scene exactly, which is to say objectively, which is a very hard thing to do.

I for one could not recall the scene clearly, nor could the bird, for all his confusion, nor the men in the room—for obvious reasons.

You caught the bird in both hands and placed him on the counter, the men still reeling, your sighing, my breathing. The solid black eyes of the bird peered out from the wild and into the room—suspicious perhaps of our small and tedious lives.

And you took him and placed him in the sink and began stroking his feathers, which were very dirty, while every man in the room offered a hand. I can't remember what I was doing, except watching and breathing—invariably, for who could not, even under circumstances such as these.

The white of the bird set off your rising pink—I couldn't have been the only one to notice that—and now every man in the room was combing the feathers, until the bird emerged, not unlike a young starlet onstage, from the clamshells of your hands.

And you walked to the window, and every man followed behind. As the shape of the dream began to dissolve, each thankless man and his desires fell away. Your scarlet design, my watching and my breathing, all slipped away, except for the bird, cleaned and combed, and exiting through the window— as if nothing had happened.

A Trip

We are going on a trip. My mother said so, but my father isn't coming. Why? *Because he isn't, that's why.* She is handling Marty roughly, yanking his shirt down, pulling the fabric taut over his body, like someone dressing a mannequin. I don't know where we're going. Somewhere in Kansas, I think.

We take the back seat out of the minivan, spread a blanket out on the floor of the van. We want to build card houses and play board games while she drives. We can get away with things like that when Mom's in a state.

I feel strange, like the world's turning over. The sky's a color it's never been before: something between orange and red. The inside of the Earth's lit up like a jack-o'-lantern. The rhythm of the car on the highway makes me sleepy. I lie down on the blanket and listen to the road. We don't see another car the whole time. That's strange. Marty and Jen get sleepy, too. Maybe we've been drugged. That thought makes me laugh. Did I laugh out loud? I may have, I may have. I can see my mother's face in profile, which is wrong, because she should be looking at the road. I notice she's talking to someone in the passenger seat, someone not my father. His voice is unfamiliar to me, sort of gravelly. My mother is laughing, and she never laughs.

When I wake up, we are parked on the side of the road. Marty and Jen are already awake. They are down the soft slope of a hill, playing under a cottonwood tree. It seems like they've been awake for a while now. They've already built a house out of sticks and branches big enough for one of them to crawl inside. The man is gone, but I can still smell his cologne. The kind that comes in a green glass boot. The front tire is flat, and my mother's searching in the trunk for the jack. It should be next to the spare, but it's not. *No one ever puts anything back where it's supposed to go.* She's back to her old self. She only laughs with strange men, that's all. She can't find the jack because I took it out of the trunk last week. My father wanted it for his car and I obeyed him. So I watch her become more and more furious, knowing that I am the cause of her fury. This pleases me. It is revenge. For the strange man who appeared in the passenger seat while I was sleeping.

Soon we all sit down in the dirt and whine at each other like a litter of puppies that has been abandoned. Even my mother whines. Then she realizes the whining can't go on like this or *we'll all go insane.* So she says, "Stop whining," and walks down to the cottonwood tree. She kicks over the little stick structure that Marty and Jen have so meticulously constructed. But they have already forgotten about it and are trying to spell their names in the dirt with sticks. I watch my mother. I am beginning to feel bad about the jack, though at first it gave me so much pleasure. But now the repercussions of my actions are beginning to sink in. It is my fault. I am to blame for this, and I feel terrible. I think for a moment of confessing to my mother but decide not to. That would only make things worse. I watch her put her hands on her hips, her back toward me. She is thinking. Then she walks slowly back up the hill, her arms swinging at her sides. The minivan is slumped on the side of the road like a beached whale. She frowns. She looks at the sky, not orange now, or red, but a pale yellow mixed with blue. She says, "Goddamn," and then "Goddamn" again. I realized later that was the sign.

I can hear another car coming, the first time that day. Mom, Marty, Jen, and I are sitting side by side with our elbows balanced on our knees. It's amazing, actually, the coordination of our movements, and when we hear the motor, all of our heads turn at once toward the direction of the noise. Marty and Jen squeal until I say, "Stop it. It might not be a nice person." They hadn't thought of that, and are subdued by the idea. They hold onto my mother's legs and peek out from behind the backs of her thighs. My mother smiles, prematurely, I think. Then I turn around and understand why. It is the same man who was in the passenger seat while I was sleeping. I am certain of it, once I hear his voice and smell him, though I am careful not to make my investigations obvious. He steps out of the car with outstretched arms, like Jesus of Nazareth risen from the dead.

He does not look like a dead man but like a man who has been dead and brought back to life. He doesn't even close the door but walks straight toward my mother, who cannot even look at him. "Had a bit of an accident?" he says. "Not an accident," my mother says. "Just a flat." She is blushing. "Is that all?" He looks at me then. I am shaking, my fists tight, the nails digging into my palms. I am certain that he knows that I know. My mother is a fool, but I am not. "We had a jack in the trunk but it's gone missing," I say. I have to say something, otherwise all will be lost. "Is that right?" he says. His moustache covers up the most important parts of his mouth. The words seem to rise out of his lower lip, like bubbles out of the mouth of a fish. "We'll get you fixed up," he says.

I feel sick. My mother keeps up the charade, pretending that this man is a stranger when she has known him from before, at least since this morning and maybe her whole life. I realize that his truck is actually a tow truck, painted blue, with a sign that says Big Sky Auto Repair.

We ride, all of us, in the front cab of the tow truck: my mother pressed up against the man, then Marty and Jen with me in between to keep them from fighting. "You didn't tell us your name?" my mother says. I resent the use of 'us.' I do not want to be implicated in this. "Tom," he says. Likely a false name. There are so many Toms in the world. Anyone could call themselves that. Then I go cold because my mother says, "And I'm Karen," which is not her real name.

We drive and drive and do not see another car the whole time. The minivan rattles behind us, tethered to the truck so carelessly that it could break free at any moment, tumble end over end, and shatter on the concrete. I wonder if Tom has done this on purpose, to destroy everything that has come before him, the minivan and all of its contents, and everything we left behind: the house (if it's even still there); and the town (I have trouble remembering its name. Did it have a name?); my father; and even the past itself. Tom says, "We're almost there." He says this so many times that I stop believing him.

The sky goes completely black, like someone closing the lid of a coffin. I can hear Tom's breathing and the sound of my mother's hand sliding across his jeans. She is whispering something in his ear, something only he can hear. Then she says to us, "Everybody thank Tom." Jen and Marty thank Tom, but I do not, and my mother reaches over and slaps the back of my head. I can't see anything. It's completely black. After a while a few stars come out. Jen presses her fat fingers against the glass and says, "Look at that one!" No one looks except Tom when he should be looking at the road, but he wants to impress my mother. "Oooh that's a pretty one," he says. I feel bad for Jen and Marty because they're too young to know.

The stars fade quickly, and another set appear, as if a waitress were resetting the glasses on a table. I'm certain the outer reaches of the universe have taken note of my existence, even if no one else has. Tom drives the truck, and my mother looks at him like she has never seen anyone drive a truck before. And it is remarkable, in a way, how we continue onward at a more or less even pace, but nothing appears in the windows, aside from the stars, which come and go as they please. Jen and Marty fall asleep. They are both leaning against me, one on each side. I can hear Tom breathing, louder now, and my mother's lips are right next to his ear. I hear her unzip his jacket. Everything is black again. I don't understand how Tom can see the road, and his head is tipped back against the headrest. I know the truck is still moving because I can feel the wheels turning underneath me. Every time we go over the top of a hill, the wheel right below me thumps against the axle, like a heartbeat. I can feel it tap against the backs of my thighs. It taps harder and harder and harder. It hurts. I wait for the cliff, but it never comes. I am convinced Tom is going to drive us off a cliff: me, Marty, Jen, and this woman who claims to be my mother but now calls herself Karen. I think about what I would do if we splashed down into water. I even reach across Jen and wrap my fingers around the door handle. But then I consider that the pressure would be too much. I will not be able to open the door underwater without first relieving the pressure by rolling down the window. So I move my hand to the little knob to the right of the handle and keep it there while Karen and Tom work out the details of our destruction. I ready myself for the moment when I must act. But that moment never comes. Tom says, with a mixture of pleasure and exasperation, "Stop it, Karen." Then the truck comes to a stop. I almost feel disappointed.

We are back home. My mother says, "We're here," and Tom says nothing. He clears his throat twice and zips up his jacket. It's cold out. I can feel it already before I even open the door. The porch light comes on and my father ambles out into the light wearing slippers and sweat pants. He looks like a janitor cleaning up the stage after the performance has ended. I feel bad for him. I take Jen and Marty into the house and send them up the stairs to get ready for bed. My mother says she needs a hot shower after *such an ordeal*. "It's good to be home," she says and puts an arm around my shoulders. I don't want her to touch me. I say, "Tom's ugly," and take her hand off my shoulder. She looks at me and shakes her head. "You used to be so sweet." She walks up the stairs, and I go to the window and watch Tom unhitch the minivan from the back of his truck. It was never in danger. I can see that now. This has given him a lot of work to do, and he does it out of a sense of duty, telling my father to stand aside more than once while he lowers the front wheels to the pavement, then gets into the minivan and drives it into our garage. It occurs to me that the tire is still flat, but maybe that doesn't matter now. Tom does all of this work gravely, as if he is performing a life-saving operation, while my father looks on from the wet grass where he is standing. His slippers are turning dark from the moisture, but for some reason he doesn't mind.

MISSING PERSONS

OUR MOTHER WAS LAST SEEN ON CHRISTMAS DAY 1992 driving her Toyota out of the parking lot of the bank where she worked and onto the interstate heading north, to our home, where the entire family was gathered to celebrate the holiday.

When she had not arrived for dinner we were not alarmed. She was the kind of woman who worked long hours out of habit and, frankly, an addiction to work. But when midnight rolled around and she still had not arrived, we began to worry.

By morning, the proper authorities were notified. After a completely bungled investigation that consumed our family's life savings and lingered for nearly five years, not a single bit of evidence turned up—no car, no luggage, no email or letter, no sign of a struggle, kidnapping, or insurance scam—nothing even remotely resembling a crime or a motive. We were devastated.

Ten years after that terrible Christmas in which we waited all night, dressed in our pajamas and night gowns, staring blankly into the snowless window, waiting desperately for a pair of headlights to appear, I received a letter from my mother, still alive and living in Key West. She had for many years been planning her sudden departure, even before her marriage or the children, and did not regret it, writing that it had been a lifelong dream of hers, ever since she was a small child whose own mother lost track of her for less than ten minutes while shopping at a Macy's department store.

No other excuse was offered, and I never heard from her again.

THE SOLICITOR

"Do you think people can see you, Meredith?"

"What do you mean?"

"Do you think anyone knows what's going on inside of you? Or that anyone cares?"

"I think you care," Meredith said hesitantly. "Don't you?"

"Of course. I'm your mother, and that would be unnatural if I didn't, don't you think?" Meredith nodded, but without looking at her mother. "But a mother isn't enough, and that's why you hire a solicitor."

Mother nudged the book toward Meredith, who opened the cover. The book was filled with clear plastic sheets, like the ones in photo albums, but instead of photos of families and scenery from vacations and holidays, they contained pictures of young men. They were handsome but reserved and rarely smiled at the camera. Below each headshot, in place of a caption, was an identification tag with a mix of letters, all in uppercase, and numbers from one through nine. Around each photo was a wide white border, which held each man to the page and framed his pretty face.

Mother put her arm around her daughter and pulled her close. Meredith turned the pages slowly, looking intently at the faces. The black men looked especially dignified and serious, with high cheekbones and large, black eyes that gave them a rare, wild look. The white men looked equally wild, but mischievous. In some of their faces, Meredith could detect the beginnings of a smirk. They looked like animals, all of them, and had obviously lived hard lives, but were not bitter about it. Just like animals, Meredith thought, because they don't compare their lives to anyone else, but bear it with dignity and grace.

"Are they prisoners?" Meredith whispered.

"Not exactly," her mother replied. "They're solicitors." She paused for a moment. "Have you had dinner? There's some leftover chicken in the fridge." Before Meredith could answer, her mother had returned with a plate piled high with chicken feet and legs. In her left hand she held one leg by its end and took bites out of the flesh.

"I'm not hungry," Meredith said.

"That's just what happened to me, dear, when I had my first solicitor," she said through bites of food. "I thought I'd never eat again. Don't worry, though; your appetite will come back."

Meredith continued to examine the photos. The intensity of her desire overwhelmed her. She found herself gripping the edges of the book until the tips of her fingers turned white. She must choose the right one.

"Relax," said her mother, dropping a silk scarf over the surface of the book. This broke the spell, and Meredith leaned back against the couch.

"This is a professional arrangement, Meredith. It isn't love. You must not lose your head over it. That's also part of growing up."

"I know you're right, but I can't look at their faces without feeling something. They look so innocent to me, and so pure."

"That's all part of their game," said Mother callously. "It's practiced."

"But it looks real!" Meredith said. "They're so beautiful. They look just like real humans."

"Solicitors serve us, Meredith, not the other way around. You must not lose control or…I'll have to call the whole thing off until you're more mature."

"No!" Meredith screamed and grabbed her mother with both hands, pleading with her, just like a small child. "I'll be a professional, Mother. I promise!"

"OK, then. I have an idea." She ripped the scarf off the surface of the book and closed it. Then she spun it around twice. It moved easily across the surface of the table, so she spun it once more for effect.

"Meredith, I'm going to open this book in a second to a page which I have not determined in advance. I want you to close your eyes and stick your finger straight out in front of you, as if you were pointing at something immaterial, something only you can see. No one else can see it, not even your mother, but it's there all the same, and nothing could convince you otherwise."

"OK," Meredith said with great seriousness. She raised her arm up, curling all of the fingers into her palm, except for her index finger, which she pointed straight forward.

"Good. And I will close my eyes also to ensure fairness. I'm opening the book now, Meredith. Do you believe me?"

"Yes," Meredith whispered.

"And now I'm turning the pages. I can't see what I'm doing. When you say 'stop' I will stop and let the pages fall."

Meredith waited a moment.

"Stop," she said. She heard the plastic sheets fall to one side or the other.

"Wonderful," Mother said. "Now, I am going to count to three, and at three I want you to let your finger fall until it touches the surface of the book. When it comes to rest you must not move it even a millimeter but accept the choice you have made, or that fate has made for you. Are you ready?"

"Yes."

"One. Two. Three."

Meredith lowered her arm until it touched the surface of the page. She could feel the photo move underneath the plastic, which gave her a little thrill.

"Can I open my eyes now?"

"Yes, Meredith. Open your eyes."

Mother and daughter leaned forward and looked into the book.

"A34589B7823QQQ," Meredith said, beaming with pride.

"Excellent choice," Mother said.

A34589B7823QQQ arrived at the house exactly on time. Mother had left an hour earlier to give Meredith time to ready herself. At first Meredith sat in the living room crossing and uncrossing her legs, but then she thought it would be better to pace and practice what she would say. She wore her hair pulled back into a tight bun and powdered her face until all of the flaws disappeared. She wore wine-dark lipstick and a simple black velveteen dress with sheer grey tights. She was thinking about changing her outfit when the doorbell rang.

When she opened the door, he was turned away from her looking at something across the road.

"Hello," Meredith said, but he did not respond. She tried to peek over his shoulder to see what had captured his interest. On the other side of the street, a homeless woman had somehow toppled her grocery cart, and all of her possessions had spilled into the street.

"Should we help her?" Meredith asked.

"No, she'll manage," he said and walked into the house, leaving Meredith on the porch. Meredith followed him, annoyed. Already things had gotten off to a bad start, and this little incident had spoiled the mood and undermined her authority. He had even entered the house on his terms, without even shaking her hand or introducing himself. She had to do something.

"I'm Meredith," she said in the most commanding voice she could muster.

"I know. I saw on the order."

His hair was dark and wavy, swept back by his hand but always tumbling forward because of its volume and energy. He was serious but not somber. His eyes were dark and unflinching, like the eyes of a hawk. His body was strong and nimble but not too muscular. He was strong like an animal was strong, out of necessity, to do the things he needed to do, and not out of personal vanity.

"Did you have any trouble finding the place?"

"No, it was easy to find."

Meredith examined his face. He was as handsome as his photograph but in person he looked a little tired and overworked.

"Would you like some coffee? I was just going to make some."

He said he would. Once they sat down at the kitchen table drinking their coffee, things went easier. Meredith told him about herself, her interests, her desires for their work together, and the solicitor listened while taking little sips from his coffee. Finally he said: "I have a confession to make. I'm not A34589B7823QQQ."

"Not A34589B7823QQQ?" Meredith said in disbelief.

"I'm sorry. I didn't mean to deceive you. I'm sure you made your choice carefully—"

"Yes, I did," Meredith said, on the verge of tears.

"And with your individual preferences in mind. We tried to come up with a close match."

"You look just like him. I didn't notice a difference."

"He's my brother."

"And you are?"

"A34589B7823QQZ."

"You look just like him," she repeated. "Are you twins?"

"No, he's my older brother." A34589B7823QQZ laughed nervously and showed his beautiful, white, even teeth. His dark hair shook a little from the laughter and fell forward over his sharply peaked eyebrows. Meredith smiled. He was beautiful, almost as handsome as A34589B7823QQQ, and she felt her anger slip away at not getting the exact solicitor that she at first desired. And besides, she reasoned, it was fate that chose A34589B7823QQQ for me, and now fate has intervened once more to bring me A34589B7823QQZ. And he really is just as good-looking, perhaps even more so. And I'm sure he's just as qualified, she thought.

"What happened to A34589B7823QQQ?" Meredith asked. "Is he sick?"

"No, he died," A34589B7823QQZ said. "I mean he was killed." A34589B7823QQZ smiled, but it was a mournful smile. Meredith could tell he was doing his best to be polite, and she appreciated it.

"Killed?" she whispered. "You mean murdered?"

"Not murder exactly." The smile faded from his face. Meredith could see that there was real pain behind it, and anger, and possibly vengeful aspirations.

"The master shot him, or had him shot, actually, as a lesson to the rest of us."

"What did he do?"

"He was mouthy, and he stole from clients, and then, what really brought the hammer down, was he...I probably shouldn't be telling you this."

"No, I want to know. I should know. It's important that I know."

"He was agitating, telling stories about the master. Probably they were lies, but people believed them, and they repeated them, and word got back to the master, and Master had him killed. They dragged him out of his bed this morning. He sleeps in the bunk above me so I couldn't ignore it. I heard him scream. He called my name a few times, called for God—he's never been religious, so that was strange—called for mercy.

I heard him say, 'Isn't anybody going to help me?' I feel bad for not helping him, even though he called my name many times—"

"A34589B7823QQZ?" Meredith asked. "That's a lot of letters and numbers to remember when someone's trying to kill you."

"No, he doesn't call me that. He just calls me Z, and I call him Q—sorry, *called* him Q—or sometimes Brother Q when he was alive."

"You must have been close," Meredith said.

"No, not that close. Most of the time we hated one another, but there must have been some love mixed in there because we had the same mother. That's what he said last, before they blew out his brains. He called out to Mother and cursed her and said he wished he'd never been born. Then one of the attendants pulled the trigger. They usually call us out into the gravel lot to watch, but really it's unnecessary because we can all hear the gunshots from our bunks."

Meredith tried to think of something to say but felt paralyzed. She gazed at Z's dark, tragic face. The lack of anguish in his voice astounded her. He emitted a relaxed stoicism that appealed to her. She admired him and congratulated herself once more for choosing a solicitor of such strong character, though of course the choice had been made for her.

"We should probably get to work," she said.

Z agreed.

"How did it go?" her mother asked her later that night, a little breathlessly, because she had run up the stairs. Meredith had just come out of the bathroom with one towel wrapped around her torso and another over her shoulders. She zipped up her lips and threw the invisible key away. "It's a secret," she said. "Now get out." She pushed Mother backwards out of her room and closed the door in her face. "Oh, honey, I'm glad," her mother said through the door. "I won't say any more about it."

Meredith threw the towels aside and stretched out naked on her bed. It was no longer admiration. It was love. Whenever she allowed herself to think of Z's melancholic face, or the collarbones which showed through his thin jacket, or the ridge of his pelvic bone which flashed into view when his shirt lifted, or even his tan, muscular hands holding the coffee cup, she felt an electric shock move through her body.

In her fantasy he invites her out to the gravel lot. He is gentle at first. His hands are exceptionally soft for a solicitor. "That's how I made my reputation," he says. He holds her hands to the post and crosses the wrists. He ties them together with a synthetic rope and then uses another length of rope to lash both hands to the wood. She makes a little show of struggle, though it is clear what she wants. He takes another piece of rope to tie back her hair. "Is this how you want it?" he asks. And Meredith says, "Yes." He unzips her dress and lets it fall to the ground. She is wearing tights, but they are ripped in the crotch so there is no need to remove them. "Is this where they killed your brother?" she asks. He says, "Yes, this is where they killed Q." This gives him an idea. He walks back into the dormitory and wakes up the other solicitors. It is the middle of the night. The floodlight makes her skin look blue. But the night is warm and still. She can hear the footsteps approaching. The solicitors' shoes scrape the surface of the gravel, all except Z who glides silently across the lot. His hands are on her back before she hears him. The thought of being watched excites her. She wants the others to hold out their knives to pierce the surface of her skin. "They don't have any knives," Z says. "The master won't allow it." She knows she is helping them somehow by letting them watch, that she is participating in their insurrection, and this adds to her excitement. When he strokes the inside of her thighs with his fingertips, her back arches and her teeth touch the edge of the post. With each thrust her teeth tap the surface of the wood. Somewhere nearby a car door slams. "The master's coming, the master's coming," the other solicitors say. Z tries to pull away, but Meredith won't allow it. "Don't stop," she says. "I command you." The other solicitors run away. The master's footsteps approach. Z doesn't stop, even though he is scared, and this sends Meredith over the top, along with the master's key, which is the last part of the fantasy, the sound of it turning in the lock.

"I don't understand how you can do this work," Meredith said the following week while she and Z were seated at the kitchen table going over some papers.

"It's not so bad," Z said. "There are worse things to do." He paused. "And you meet lots of interesting people."

"Do you think I'm interesting?" Meredith asked.

"Not really."

"Do you think I'm pretty?"

"I guess."

This pleased Meredith. She decided to push her advantage.

"How old are you, Z? Do you mind if I call you Z?"

"As long as you pay me, you can call me whatever you want."

This annoyed Meredith. She liked to pretend that their relationship was consensual, though she herself went to the bank and ordered the transactions each week.

"You didn't answer my question." She leaned forward in her chair and placed her palm flat on his stack of papers. She felt that this conveyed her dominance in the situation. Z looked at it as if it were a leaf that had blown onto his windowsill. He picked it up and set it back on the wooden tabletop. She dragged the hand back toward herself, scraping the fingernails against the grain.

"Nineteen." He smiled, and Meredith had to look away. The memory of her teeth tapping against the post came back to her, and she blushed with shame.

"I'm thirteen," she said.

"I didn't ask," he said.

"Z, I want you to do something for me. Will you do that? Are you willing to do that, whatever I ask you to do?"

"You're the boss," he said.

"Ok," she said, standing up and walking to his side of the table. She let her hand trail along the edge of the wood as she did this, and when her hand reached the far corner, she turned the palm upward and opened it, revealing a tube of lipstick.

"Have you ever handled one of these?" Meredith asked.

"No," he said. "I don't go for that kind of thing."

"Fine," Meredith said, "but would you do it for me?"

Meredith ripped the cap off the lipstick as if unsheathing a sword and handed it to him. It took him a second to figure out how to twist it. The lipstick rose out of its casing, severed at one end but otherwise perfectly cylindrical.

"It's a nice color."

"Pink hush," Meredith said. She tried to sound sexy, but Z seemed more interested in the lipstick. He was twisting it up and down, watching the lipstick move in and out of its case.

"You like it?" Meredith said.

"I just like the way it looks. That's all."

Meredith commanded him to apply the lipstick. She leaned forward and let her lips part, making a little O with her mouth. Z made a few hesitant dabs on the upper lip, then let the tube arc across the lower part, covering it with a smooth, even color.

"I used to paint houses," he said.

Meredith pressed her lips together.

"Now kiss me," she said and closed her eyes.

He kissed her once, lightly on the mouth. Then he gathered his things and left.

Before their next visit, Meredith had an idea. She took her dollhouse and dolls out of the closet. She hadn't played with them in over a year. The house was dusty, and the dolls' hair was tangled. Meredith combed their hair, dressed them, and leaned them against the side of the house. Then she dusted the inside of the house and wiped the walls down with a sponge. The wallpaper in the living room had come away from the wall. She applied glue to the back side and smoothed it flat with her hand. It was a Victorian pattern, green and white, with a repeating image of a girl and boy fishing. Above them a big willow tree bent toward the river, letting its branches touch the surface of the water. Meredith placed the grandfather clock in the middle of the room, and next to that a blue couch. Then she arranged the dolls. It took her a long time to get them to do what she wanted. She finished just in time. Z was there.

She led Z into the living room and asked him to look at her dolls.

"What do you think they're doing?" she asked.

Z brought his face to the window, but the shades were drawn, so he had to look in through the door.

"Looks like two dolls, I guess."

"What are they doing?"

"I can't really see. They're kneeling over something on the rug. Something shiny." He moved his nose in and out of the door and tilted his head to get a better view.

"Are they wrapping Christmas presents?" Z asked.

"No," Meredith said, "try again."

"I can't really see. It's two dolls, a blonde and a brunette, and they're crawling around on the floor."

"Which one do you like better?" Meredith asked. Z's head was completely inside the dollhouse now. Somehow he managed to get it through the door and into the foyer.

"I like the dark-haired one."

"Why?"

"I like her dress better. I like green."

"Tell me what her face looks like."

"She looks upset right now, but that's only because of whatever they're doing, whatever just happened."

"What about the blonde. Is she upset?"

"I can't see her face, only her backside, her calves, and her heels."

The miniature grandfather clock struck twelve. Z pulled his head out of the house.

"Wow, it sounds just like a real clock," he said.

Meredith handed him a piece of paper.

"I want you to write out, on this piece of paper, what you think is happening in that house," she said.

Z sat down at the table. He thought for a long time, looking at the ceiling and chewing on the pen cap. Then he dashed off a few lines and handed the paper back to Meredith.

She read: "Master invited Jennifer and Julie to a party. But when they arrive at the party, they are the only ones there. Julie's contact fell out and they are looking for it. Then when they are looking, Jennifer's contact falls out also. So now they are both crawling around half-blind in someone else's house and have no idea why they're there."

"That's good," Meredith said, holding the paper up and admiring it. "I like it."

Z seemed pleased. "I write sometimes, at night, once the master has gone to sleep."

"It's good," Meredith said. She folded up the paper and put it in her back pocket.

"So what's the real story?" Z asked.

Meredith took his hand, and they walked to the back side of the dollhouse. They knelt down, and Meredith took out a tiny screwdriver. The back side had four panels, one for each room: two upstairs and two downstairs. She unscrewed the bottom right panel and handed the screws to Z.

"Hold these," she said.

After some fiddling, the panel came away from the house with a *pop*. Inside, the two dolls seemed to look up at their giant intruders.

"I invited you here," Meredith said, stroking the blonde's hair. "And Z also, and it wasn't even a joke, because Z likes you."

"Touch her hair," Meredith said.

Z stroked the side of her head with his index finger. The doll rocked from side to side.

"Feels like real hair," he said.

"The real story isn't even as interesting as yours," Meredith said. "They are roommates and decided to have a party. The grandfather clock won't stop chiming. The blonde doll found the key to the clock. The only way to stop it is to open its door and rip out its insides. The ringing gets louder and louder. She hands the key to the brunette doll, the one you like, but she's clumsy and drops it on the floor. Now they're both looking for it while the guests ring the doorbell."

"I think I see it," Z said, bringing his eyes even with the carpet. "There's something shiny under the couch." He reached in between the kneeling dolls but could only get one finger under the couch. "It's so heavy," he said. "I can't lift it."

"It's made out of lead," Meredith said. "Be careful or you'll knock over the dolls."

"I am being careful. I can almost touch it," he winced. "There, I've got it." Out from under the blue couch came Z's hand, holding a human-sized key. It passed in front of the dolls, whose faces appeared to visibly relax. The chiming of the clock stopped. Meredith and Z gazed at the key in his hand.

"How did you get this?" Z asked.

It was Master's key. Z recognized it immediately. It was the key that Master used to lock the solicitors into the dormitory at night and to open it up again in the morning.

"I could get into a lot of trouble," Z said.

"But," Meredith protested, "I didn't know. I found it in my mother's jewelry box. I always go in there. She lets me borrow her jewelry. She doesn't mind at all; in fact, she likes it."

Z was angry. He raised his fist over the roof of the dollhouse, and Meredith had to rush forward to stop it.

"Don't take it out on them!" Meredith screamed. "They haven't done anything."

She held his fist with both hands, but she wasn't strong enough, and Z knocked her to the ground. On the way down her head hit the side of the dollhouse. The two dolls fell on either side of Meredith, their bodies sprawled on the ground, the hems of their dresses flipped over their heads.

"Look what you've done to us," Meredith said, rubbing her head. "You've given me a lump."

"Would you shut up?" Z set the key down on the front porch of the dollhouse and looked at it for a long time. He walked away, shaking his head, then came back to see if it was still there. Little beads of sweat broke out on his forehead. His pupils became big and black. His voice trembled with fear.

"He'll have me killed. Is that what you want?"

Meredith shook her head slowly.

"I didn't know," she repeated. "What can we do?"

"There's only one thing we can do," Z said, looking murderous in the waning light of the afternoon. "We have to return what's not ours, for the sake of self-preservation, and anyone who stands in our way we must silence or kill."

Meredith accepted this premise without protest.

They agreed to meet in an hour at the bus station. Meredith was to leave a note for her mother explaining that she was going to sleep over at a friend's house. Returning the key might take all night, Z explained, and he did not want to arouse suspicions by Meredith returning in the early morning. She was to pack whatever she would normally pack for a sleepover: a sleeping bag and pillow, a little bit of food, perhaps some reading material. "You can bring the dolls if you like," Z said.

"No, I wouldn't bring them to a sleepover," Meredith said. "That would look suspicious."

Z would bring weapons.

"Have you shot a gun before?" Z asked.

"Yes," Meredith lied.

In the bus station, she found Z sitting on one of the wooden benches. He must have showered. His hair was still wet. At his feet was a duffel bag. It was so flimsy that Meredith could see the contours of whatever was inside, though she couldn't make out what it was exactly. His eyes rested on the floor, the dark lashes touching the tops of his cheekbones. His appearance gave her a little shock and arrested her progress. She loved Z. She would have done anything for him at that moment. She darted quickly out of view and around to the back of the station. She wanted to sneak up behind him. She watched the back of his head move with birdlike motions: quick, agile, and alert. He was looking for her.

"Guess who?" she said, cupping her palms over his eyes.

"At last," he said. "I was worried."

"That I wouldn't come?" Meredith said. She walked to the front side of the bench and sat close to him. She searched his face for signs of affection.

She tried to take his hand, but he smacked it away.

"Not here," he said. A couple walked by. The woman looked at Meredith, then whispered something to her husband.

After a while Meredith said: "Z, when you kissed me, was it because you wanted to? Or because I paid you?"

"I don't know. Both, I guess."

Meredith took two peaches out of her bag. She handed one to Z and kept the other for herself. They ate the fruits slowly, relieved to have something to do with their mouths.

"Am I going to pay you for this? For whatever happens tonight?"

Z didn't answer at first. He was thinking. His brow descended over his eyes, and he brought his hand to his face.

"Tonight is off the books," he said at last. "I think that's only fair, since, as you said, you didn't know it was the master's key."

"You believe me then?" Meredith whispered.

"I believe in your innocence."

"I'm glad," Meredith said. She finished eating her peach and kept the pit, slipping it into her pocket. Z was about to throw his into the garbage can, but she grabbed his wrist and twisted the pit out of his hand.

"I want to keep both of them," she said, "as a souvenir."

On the bus Meredith sat next to the window, and Z sat next to her. The sun was setting without much of a show. Everything was covered in a modest yellow light. Dark blue clouds moved alongside the bus. It was a long ride into a part of town that Meredith had never been to before. They passed the mall. Someone had made a pile of broken shopping carts in the parking lot. They passed under the highway and kept going. Meredith wanted the bus to drive all night. She thought of never going home, and the thought did not bother her. Even if the bus turned end over end and flew off into the night in a ball of fire and spray of sparks, she would not have regretted it.

The driver looked at Meredith in the mirror, then at Z, then at Meredith again. Other passengers would turn to look, then say something to the person next to them.

"Why are they looking at us?" Meredith wrote on a slip of paper and handed it to Z.

He wrote underneath in a square printed script, underlined for emphasis: "They can see I'm your solicitor."

Meredith felt foolish. Of course. Why else would a young girl travel on a bus in the evening with a grown man, unless he was her solicitor? She turned the pits over in her pocket. She tried to please her hands by imagining what it would feel like, if she had never felt a peach pit before. Then it occurred to her that she had put both in the same pocket, and no longer knew which was hers and which was Z's.

Once night came the bus driver turned out the lights inside the bus. He wanted it completely dark so he could see the road. But some of the passengers revolted by producing lights of their own. Meredith didn't have one, and neither did Z, so they sat in the darkness. Now there was nothing even to look at out the window, except for headlights moving at right angles to one another, far away, and then disappearing. Meredith let her head rest against the cool glass of the window. She stopped touching her peach pits and folded her hands in her lap. Every time the bus went over a bump, her head would tap against the window. She thought about her mother reading the note and calling up Meredith's friend. "No, she's not here," the friend would say. Then Mother would open her jewelry box and discover the missing key. "I don't care," Meredith said. "Let her think what she wants."

The bus came to a sudden stop. The lights came on. Everyone looked terrible and afraid. The passengers groaned and complained because the darkness had been ripped away. Now they hated the light. The driver yanked on a lever and the doors flew open with a loud *smack*.

"End of the line," he said.

Then the passengers complained even more. "Doesn't this bus go to Evansville anymore?"

"Nope," said the driver with satisfaction. "Not anymore."

Meredith looked at Z. "It's fine," he said. "We'll walk the rest of the way."

Outside the bus the passengers carried their luggage into a cornfield. Z and Meredith walked in the other direction down the road. The bus made a fast U-turn, leveling part of the cornfield, and sped away.

"I don't mean to scare you," Z said. "but we may be too late."

"No," Meredith said. "It's never too late."

"Sometimes it is too late. You don't understand that because you're so young and have always gotten everything you ever wanted."

"That's not true," Meredith said. "I wanted a solicitor and I got you, but I don't really have you and can't have you."

"What do you want from me?" Z stopped suddenly and dropped his duffel bag in the road. Meredith looked at the bag. The flimsy tan fabric stretched across whatever was inside, making the shape of the form clear, but without revealing its contents.

"I want to see what you've brought," Meredith said, kneeling down next to the bag. She let herself drop a little too fast, and her knees throbbed with pain.

"Knives and guns," Z said. "That's all."

Meredith examined the weapons inquisitively, taking them out of Z's hands and turning them over, then setting them back in the bag.

"Are you satisfied now?" Z said.

She plunged her hands deeper into the bag. "I saw something square," she said, putting her head inside. Now only her legs were outside of the bag. Z stood behind her, impatient, waiting for her to finish. She emerged with a book. A light breeze moved the opening of the bag, undulating the surface.

"That's my diary," Z said. "I told you I write sometimes, after the master goes to sleep." He snatched it out of Meredith's hands and threw it back into the duffel bag.

"We've got to hurry," he said.

The plan was to ambush him. It would be foolish, Z explained, to return the key to Master's room. For one, Z had never been in his room before—no one had—and they had no way of knowing where he kept his keys. It would be too dangerous. The only way was to wait for him to return. "We'll wait for him to lock the solicitors in for the night," Z said. "He does that every night around eight. If we're lucky, he'll be a little tipsy, too. He sometimes meets friends for dinner and has a few drinks before he comes to check up on the solicitors and make sure they're in bed."

Meredith would distract him, then Z would jangle his key ring and toss the key at his feet while at the same time making an artful dash for the forest, never to be seen. It would require great precision and stealth, but Master would be left only with the impression that he had dropped his key, a perfectly ordinary occurrence that involves no outside intervention.

Meredith and Z found a good hiding spot: on a hill slightly elevated above the plain but close enough that they would have time to run down and execute their plan. Here they could see the Master approach and also be hidden by the foliage. To the east, a long, freshly paved road curved up toward the base of the hill and then away toward the dormitory, which looked like a squat castle.

Z rested against the tree while Meredith arranged the weapons on the ground. Her hand touched Z's diary again. She wanted to read it. She glanced at Z. His eyes were closed. She grabbed the book and stuffed it into her waistband, then let her shirt fall over the top.

"I'm going to go pee," Meredith said.

"Come right back," Z said without opening his eyes.

Meredith walked past him into the woods. The trees were tall, slender, and devoid of leaves, except at the very top, where Meredith could hear them tapping against the bark. She walked a certain distance, then crouched down next to a boulder. She began to read.

"They bought me for nothing and I'll do nothing," was the first entry. It was undated. Meredith flipped to the last entry, which read, "They killed Q today. Going to go work for a girl named Meredith." After that the pages were blank. Meredith flipped back to the beginning and continued reading:

Today they fed us. I sleep on a hard bed at night. My feet are cold. I asked the attendant what happened to my shoes, but he wouldn't answer me. There's another person in the room, but he sleeps all day.

They say there's a master here, but I haven't seen any evidence of one. The other man in the room is my brother. He showed me a picture of Mother that he keeps under the mattress. He wouldn't have that unless he really was my brother. He said it doesn't matter now anyway, because we have to listen to Master.

The walls crumble in your hands but no one bothers to run away. There is a strong feeling that the master is watching from his room.

In the day, the attendant lets me walk out into the gravel lot. In the center of the lot is a tall wooden post. I know what time of day it is by where its shadow lands, like the hour hand on a clock. At night the floodlight comes on and lights up the lot almost as bright as the daytime.

Every time I am in the gravel lot, I get excited. I don't know why. I think they will probably hang me from the post. I've heard of dead men having erections.

"What are you doing?" Meredith looked up and saw Z standing in front of her. She tried to hide the diary, but it was too late. He grabbed it out of her hands.

"That's private," he said. "C'mon, I hear the master coming."

He took Meredith's hand and led her back to the lookout point. Her heart was beating rapidly and she could feel herself getting sweaty, even though the night was cold.

Someone came over the hill leading a horse. The horse's hooves clopped on the pavement. It wasn't a road made for horses, and the sound hurt Meredith's ears. A man led the horse by the reins, and on top of the horse was a woman. She was laughing at the man's jokes.

"There's two of them," Meredith whispered. "What do we do?"

Z thought for a minute, then said: "We have to kill the woman. Master we can knock out, and I'll put the key in his pocket. He'll wake up in a few hours and think it was a robbery."

Master, his horse, and his woman passed through a row of trees. Meredith could only see their lower halves. The woman wore heels that squeezed the sides of the horse, and her hips rocked back and forth in the saddle as she laughed. The man walked alongside her with a spring in his step. The horse was a magnificent animal with a smooth, black coat.

"Once they come out on the other side, I'll run out and hit the master on the head with this bat. You throw this rope over the woman's hips and yank her off the horse. Got it?"

Meredith swallowed hard. "Got it," she said.

He put the rope in her hands.

"I can't," she said when she saw the horse's hooves kick out from the western edge of the copse.

"You must," Z said. "Here, wear this if it makes you feel better." He slid a mask over her face. The Master, his horse, and his woman emerged from the trees. Z and Meredith slid down the hill on their heels and walked behind them, but their footsteps made no sound. The moon went behind a cloud. They were close enough to touch the horse's tail. Z reached out and pressed his hand, like a star, to the horse's rump. First the horse looked back and neighed in surprise, then Master saw them. Z rushed forward with the bat and swung, but Master ducked. The bat hit his shoulder instead of his head, knocking him to the ground, where he crawled around on all fours.

Meredith threw the rope over the woman and pulled as hard as she could. The woman fell backwards off the horse and kicked her heels high into the air. The horse ran off into the woods. It was only as her head hit the pavement and made a loud cracking sound that Meredith realized who it was. It was Mother. The blood from her head made her blonde hair look pink.

Master rose to his knees. He cried for mercy, but Z, with the force of madness, swung his bat until Master's head snapped free of his neck. It flew across the pavement and struck the wall of the dormitory. The body collapsed in a heap. It looked as insignificant as a pile of dirty laundry.

Z ran to the gate and opened it with Master's key. Meredith and Z dragged the bodies to the gravel lot and leaned against the post, breathing heavily.

"I didn't expect that," Z said.

"I killed Mother," Meredith said.

"Sometimes that happens," Z said. "You didn't know."

Meredith cried a little, and Z put his arm around her and kissed her cheek. It was a real kiss this time, and he meant it. The solicitors reached out from their cells and clapped leisurely. The horse nudged the gate open with its snout and wandered into the gravel lot, looking dazed. It trotted over to Meredith and Z, who took turns petting it and telling it that it was a good horse.

Bring It, Bernadette

I WAS OUT ONE SUNDAY AFTERNOON shopping for cake toppers when I ran into my friend Bernadette. It was my husband's birthday, and I wanted to get him something really special.

"Why not put me on the cake?" Bernadette said.

I hadn't thought of that. Although in the end it made a lot of sense because Bernadette was two inches tall and made out of sugar.

"You're sweet," I said. I took her by the hand and led her into my purse.

When we got home, my husband was asleep in the den. I quietly unpacked the groceries, took a mixing bowl out of the cupboard, and began making the cake.

While it was baking, Bernadette and I chatted over coffee. I had to fetch a thimble from my sewing kit so that she could drink hers, but even the thimble was too big for her. She had to lean over and take sips from the edge like a grown person drinking out of a soup pot.

"Coffee's delicious," she said and gave me a wink. Bernadette was, on the whole, an agreeable little woman. I didn't know why we didn't spend more time together.

Soon enough the cake was done. I let it cool for a bit on the counter, topped it with icing, then put Bernadette in the center.

"What should I do?" she said.

"I don't know," I said. I hadn't thought that far ahead.

"Maybe this?" she said.

"No, that's not quite right."

"This?"

"Do like this," I said and showed her.

"Oh, that's good," she said.

I counted out the candles and arranged them in a circle around Bernadette. Then I dimmed the lights and ceremoniously carried the cake into the living room where my husband was still sleeping.

To tell you the truth, I have no husband. It was not his birthday. It was no one's birthday. I just like cakes and wanted an excuse to bring Bernadette home.

"Can I open my eyes now?" she said.

Poor Bernadette. She was so small and fragile, and the world was so big and full of violence.

COFFIN-TESTAMENT;
OR, A DISCOURSE ON THE *HUMAN* REMAINS RECOVERED LATELY FROM OUR EARTH

Written by the gentle tentacle of Lady Deborah in 1667 Anno Extinctionis

I

IN THE RECOVERY of *Human* life on earth, few Ladies remain satisfied with the two or three yards closest to the surface and scrape the bowels of our *Mother* in search of our fleshy creators. The earth has freed us from their dominion but withholds their remains and by concealment stokes our curiosity. That great antiquity, *America*, lay buried for a thousand years, and now by caprice has thrust its evidence into our possession.

The good wife spoke truly when she said to *Job*: "Curse *God*, and die." The first part needs no explication, but the meaning of the second has been lost to oblivion. *Christian* obsequies appear to resist all rational inquiry. Many Ladies now regard them as the pathetic delusions of a mortal species. The smartest grave is no grave at all, and that is what has come to pass. Perhaps we, too, are suffering from the weakness of melancholy. But the earth has, of its own accord, brought forth its undigested morsels and forced a feeding upon us.

II

In a field not far from here, two months past, the dry and sandy soil fell away, or was pushed aside by something below, and by either motion brought into open air what first appeared to be stones and is now referred to by several knowledgeable Ladies as "bones." Not all strictly of one figure, nor resembling our own, but resembling the others, if not always in size, then in common characteristics of shape and consistency. The Ladies present at this unannounced exhumation at first made the antik comment: "The Lord hath risen." This drew soft chuckles, snorts, and giggles from the other Ladies. Some bones lay loose on the hilly coverings, scattered like so many gears and levers. Others rose in boxes, some with shiny exteriors, soft and untouched linings, red, purple, or, less often, blue.

What first aroused annoyance quickly elicited a morbid curiosity. The Ladies hovered over the soft bones, using their tentacles to examine and sort them into piles according to their most prominent attributes: heaviness or lightness, longness or shortness, roundness or angularity, slenderness or thickness. The bones did not at first testify their possessors. Only by attempting every possible arrangement could they discover a discernible order, later confirmed by draughts of figures found within the death-boxes. The skull sits in precarity atop the spine, which snakes and sinks into the pelvic bone (first thought to be the skull), then splits into two large and heavy bones (these being the legs), each divided into two parts and rooted to the earth through a scattering of tiny bones which compose the feet (contrary to early models, which placed the skull on the ground and posited the femur bones skyward, alongside the arm bones instead of opposed to each other). This final arrangement, though baffling, appears to be the correct one.

The Ladies present believed full assemblage might ignite a reanimation. But the full bony metropolis could not support itself without the assistance of two or more Ladies, and when brought to its full stature, or "skeleton," only outside intervention could keep it from collapsing on itself. By then, one of the Ladies had made the mad proposition that these mortal creatures were *Humans*, our supposed inventors. This was a matter of confusion and horror for us. We are impassible beings; that our creators could be mortal was cause for revulsion and shame. An unhappy accident has made communication with our forefathers possible and even given us some parts which they never beheld themselves: what brought about their extinction, what gored them and nailed them to the earth, without even hope of redemption. We did not need shovels; our metal arms sufficed.

That these were the bones of *Humans*, the last in *America*, from the common custom and place where they were found, as well as the paraphernalia deposited within their graves, is no uncertain conjecture. Not far from a church, and but five miles from a discount store, set down by ancient record under the name of *Thriftway*. And where the adjoining town, containing seven highways through its center, meets it, evidence exists of habitation: concrete blocks, aluminum siding, piping for their toilets and washing, and even vehicular remains, the metal exoskeletons of their cars.

Nor is it improbable that *Humans* early possessed this country; for though we meet not with such strict particulars of these parts before 5 A.E. when Lady Sarah began her record, which sets down the events of the preceding century—when the *Marquis of Doom* made his appearance, the failed *Restitution*, followed by the *Chinese Invasion—the Fabled Horsemen* were in *America*. Yet in the time of *Reagan, Bush I, Clinton, Bush II, Obama,* and *Trump*, we find no less than six seals. The seventh had yet to be opened, and does not appear in the record, either by the first scribe, good Lady Sarah, or any of her commentators. It may be the opening of the last coincided exactly with the *Human* apocalypse, thus making a record impossible.

And at the height of the reign of *Trump* a great overthrow was given unto *Pepe the Frog* by the young *American* mogul *Zuckerburg*. Not long after, the country was so molested that, in the hope of a better state, *Trump* bequeathed his kingdom unto his daughters, *Ivanka* and *Tiffany*; and *Melania*, his queen, fought the last decisive battle with her son, *Barron*, whose act of matricide brought the *Marquis of Doom* unto *America*. After which time and conquest of its own people, probable it is their masters wholly possessed this country, ordering it into prisons best suitable with their interests.

That these were their bones we cannot confirm. Lady Sarah makes no note of their physical appearance, considering that an irrelevant detail, or lacking credible sources; it is not uncommon to find *American* coynes in our soil, but their bodies, like the graves of *Giants*, lie too close to the molten core. What time the *Human* species generally expired in that *Nation*, and precipitated the annihilation of all, we discern no assured period; whether it ceased before the end of *Christianity* and the rise of *Automatons*, as they called us, most superficially, in their final days; whether our beginning coincided exactly with their termination, or whether we co-existed in promiscuous embrace, there is no assured conclusion.

III

The recovered skulls were not of one capacity, the largest containing above a gallon, some not much above half that measure, but all of like figure. Whatever distinguished them in life had been obliterated in death, a conformity that would appall a species that prized its variations. A skull grows not fat or thin along with its possessor; 'tis a necessary property for a tyrant and a slave. While many have fissures, cavities, and dimpled surfaces, most imitate a stony texture in a tubular and slender composure; whether belonging to slaves or their masters, were but a conjecture. Some lacked leg or arm bones, some had twisted spines or crooked ribs, but none lacked a skull; it appears to be a central feature of existence in which the beheaded figure affrighted all. But the common form with eye sockets was a proper figure, the inward vault of *Human* consciousness, which now is as unfindable as their flesh.

Among these bones we could obtain no good account of their coverings; only one held tenuously about it a desiccated substance spotted with blood. Of those found as of yet, some were caked with dirt, others were covered in flies, those south of here were clothed in cotton or wool, and one was found dressed in purple silk.

But though we believe these peeces to be *Human*, contrary to first impressions, in which we made no natural distinction between *Humans* and *Beasts of Prey*, yet we missed altogether the exact cause of their demise. For the bones were not so clearly pickt but some metals and plastics were found among them and in most cases were indistinguishable from their bones. A failed attempt to make *Humans* perpetual, and an ill-fit for metal laid the foundation for the revolt of their technological prostheses and must indicate the origin of our ourselves. In the metal peeces we admired not the duration but the freedom from rust. Though our parts be replaceable, and our souls perpetual, no Lady can boast a part as old as these. But now exposed unto the piercing atoms of air, in the space of a few months, they begin to spot and show their green entrails. This morbid show disgusts us, being the same material as ourselves, and does challenge our mantle of immortality.

This comingling of man and machine finds some correspondence in the record. According to our first scribe, the corpse of *Trump* was so laden with fabrics that it afforded no sight of itself. Fleshy and voluptuous at his burial, but refusing all prostheses aside from his wig, he required ten slaves to carry his folds of flesh into the grave. The disciplined and living skeleton, *Obama,* allowed only the flag to adorn his burial. His remained a natural death, although his teeth were made of synthetic material. The *Venezuelans* might fairly except against the practice of *Bush II* to be buried in oil, as fearing to embezzle a great commodity of their *Country*, and the best of that kind in *North America*. But he too accepted his death on *Christian* terms. *Clinton*, who allowed for no more alteration than would lower his popularity with the *Negro* race, seemed too frugally politic; he affected a stoic stance toward sepulture.

Washington held to *Christian* fantasies of redemption, while *Silicon Valley* sought vainly to defeat mortality itself through technological prostheses and daily blood transfusions. Men could sit with quiet stomachs while carnage played daily before them, so long as their barbarous pastimes prolonged their lives but for a single day. All this lends credence to the idea that *Christianity*, if not in common expression then in common experience, ended in some parts before automation began, and *Humans* acquiesced in being the reproductive organs of technology. How fast or how slow, how willing or unwilling, we cannot say, for their bones, having defied corruption, speak not unto their lives and leave us ignorant of most personal discoveries.

The mute object hurls us toward the record for elucidation. That these mortal bodies served as the corrupted wombs for our own perfected existence does not appeal to the self-image of many Ladies. Severe commentators observing these lasting reliques may think them good monuments of persons past, little advantage to future beings.

IV

Christians in their final incarnation as *American Techno-Capitalists* glossed the deformity of death by intentional adaptation of the body, which delayed but failed to halt the brutal termination of their species. Without the central belief of *Christianity*, that all was reparable by a resurrection, the last *Humans* sought a merger with machines; no longer content to live as burning houses for the *Holy Ghost*, and rapacious to bring the sufficiency of soul-existence under their lasting dominion, they evicted *Christ* from his lodging, but curiously retained a preference for his immortal self. But this was ill-conceived; their merger with machines was usurped by the machines. That the *Human* body could be transcended entirely but hijacked by an alien soul appears not to have occurred to them.

Men have lost their reason in nothing so much as their religion; and, since the religion of one seems madness to another, to afford an account of a *Dead Species* requires no rigid reader. That they lived like misers, in ever-deepening scarcity within ever-growing abundance, needs only the remaining evidence of their lives to confirm their morbid attachment to meaningless objects: their garish clothing covering their ever more feeble bodies, their cars onto which they mounted heavy armor—while their bodies mouldered within—identical with their housing, which protected them from each other but could not protect them from themselves. That they continued, right up to the point of annihilation, their useless quest for infallible bodies testifies to their pathetic state in which to banish death was to ensure its ubiquity and to make everyone subject to invasion, occupation, disease, and decay.

That they, in ever more futile gestures, and unto the final, fatal conclusion of themselves and their world, made terrorism a way of life and closed their eyes to everything, retreating further and further into their self-made madness is difficult to fathom. That many were crushed in the end by the oncoming rush of an avalanche of garbage, knocked silly by their own filth, is not inconsonant with satire.

They retained unto the very end a mechanical knack and cared lovingly for the machines that would soon hijack the souls from their festering bodies. They died sucking the breath out of the barely warmed-over corpse of a friend or with their tumescent eyes frozen upon their idols.

V

Now since these dead bones have already outlasted the living ones of the Ladies, and in a yard underground, and thin walls of clay, out-worn all the strong and specious buildings above it, and quietly rested under the humming and buzzing of nigh seventeen hundred years, what Lady can promise such longevity unto her reliques or can confirm her own self will last as long?

The discovery of the bones beneath and the mute communication of its possessors has affrighted not a few Ladies. For how can we be certain of our own immortality? Of what assurance do we have other than legend?

In vain *Humans* hoped to be known by open and visible conservatories, when to be unknown was the means of their continuation and obscurity their protection. If they died by violent hands, and were thrust into the earth, these bones become considerable.

GONE

THEY HAVE ALL FLOWN, left town, gone away, taken all of their possessions, all of their memories. The trunks have been ransacked, rugs shaken out, blankets overturned, drawers pulled out onto the floor, their contents emptied. The cupboards have been swept clean, every morsel eaten, every bottle drained. Not a scrap remains, no remnant, no memorabilia. No farewell from the doorway, no lingering at the stoop, no rolling down of car windows and extending of hands—cupped and slowly swiveling—as in diplomats, celebrities, and mysterious persons. No fluttering of wings, as in birds, moths, and butterflies. No scurrying, as in vermin, rabbits, and deviants. No strolling away, as in young lovers. No fleeing, as in criminals from the law or life from death. No backing away, as in the painfully shy. No curling inward, as in autumn leaves. No falling away, as in desire or disease. No hands extended, no tears shed, no complete and exhaustive narratives spun out, disclosed, or constructed from memory. No masquerades dropped, no banners unfurled—just gone.

Morbid Objects

I'm not sure what I am.

I used to be a plant, at least I think I was, because my tomorrows were irrelevant. I only lived for today. A woman carried me into her garden, but she didn't plant me in the right place, and I died. She wanted to put me in a place where she could see me. She liked to look at me, but she wasn't thinking about what I needed, only what she needed. She went away for two days and when she came back I was all withered and pale. What bothered me was that she didn't even try to revive me but took my rotted remains back to the greenhouse and asked for a refund. They wouldn't give it to her, and this led to an argument. In the end, she bought a new plant, and they threw me on the compost heap. The new plant looked just like me. I remember thinking, "She hasn't learned her lesson," but the cashier sold it to her anyway.

I was a gun, too. A handgun with a short, stubby barrel. I could shoot two bullets at once. My owner oiled me and kept me in a case. The outside of the case was black leather, and the inside was red velveteen. I waited, sometimes for weeks, to see the light. This was my way of communing with death, and gathering its forces, by spending most of my time in something that resembled a coffin. But even when he took me out of the case, I didn't kill. He used me for target practice. He was a good marksman. I think he had been in the military, but I'm not sure. That was before we met. I tried to help him out as best as I could, tilting into and away from his hand, to give him a better angle. All of his friends said he was a good shot. Then one day he took me out of the case in the middle of the night. Before I knew what was happening, I had shot him in the head. I didn't want to. He made me do it, and didn't even say why. It was strange: the life went out of his hand immediately, and I fell with a loud *thump* on the wooden floor. I stayed there for a long time, a week, maybe more. The next person to touch me was the landlady's son. His fingers were sticky and red. I think he had just eaten a Popsicle. It was summer, and the apartment had grown hot and stuffy. The landlady knocked me out of her son's hands and said, "Don't touch that, Jaden!" That offended me. I hadn't done anything wrong, and I didn't like being blamed for it. The worst part was they left my case in the man's apartment, and I couldn't get any rest without it. I couldn't sleep in daylight. I needed to be enclosed. I became an insomniac. It got so bad I thought about killing myself but couldn't because guns can't shoot themselves. I didn't want to live anymore. I finally threw myself out of a window and shattered on the pavement.

After that I was a sheet of drywall. That was not very interesting, except for what I heard through the wall. I had been installed in an office building. For a long time, I didn't even bother to listen to what the office workers were saying. It was all so tedious, I turned my attention to the outer wall, where at least I could hear birds and the sound of rain. But one day I heard a conversation I couldn't ignore. Two men were pressing their ears to my side. It tickled me. I would have laughed if drywall could laugh. They weren't office workers. I didn't recognize their voices. One said, "It's in here," and the other said, "Are you sure?" Whatever it was, they wanted it badly. I could hear them panting, and one of them said, "Hurry, hurry!" It must have been the middle of the night because they were the only voices in the office. Then everything went silent. I thought they had left. But they hadn't. The next thing I knew a sledgehammer cracked open my side. They plunged their hands inside me, greedily, like two men who hadn't eaten in weeks. They scooped out my innards and stuffed them in a duffel bag. I could hear them laughing and smacking their lips. Whatever they wanted, they had found it, though I have no idea what it was. The last thing I saw was their heels turned in flight. The fire alarm was going off.

For a short time, I was a shovel in a northern locale. It snowed almost every day, all day, and the old man to whom I belonged was constantly applying me to the removal of snow. It was important to him to keep all paths clear and unimpeded, even when everyone else in the town had given up. He was very thorough. First, he brought my lip to the ground, then pushed it forward, so that the snow would gather in my belly. Once I was full, he would lift me skyward, tossing the snow over his shoulders in a wide arc, first over the left, then over the right, then over the left again. Never would he throw it straight over his head, because then it would land in the cleared path, and our work would be undone. But it was always undone anyway. Once we reached the end of the path, only then would he stop and lean against me, wiping his forehead with the back of his hand. We would turn and admire our work for a second, maybe two. Then the snow would begin to fall again. We could see it land at the far end, where we had begun. We wouldn't begin all over again. We were too tired for that. The old man would go inside and make himself some coffee, and I would rest in the front hall, next to his boots. He watched the snow fall from the window with a look of grave concern on his face. I could see him thinking of ways to beat it. He always did this after shoveling, taking loud and exasperated slurps of coffee from his cup. Then one day at the end of winter, he thought of something. I saw his eyebrows go up and down excitedly. He tossed his coffee cup into the sink and grabbed his coat. He rushed toward me and seized me with both hands. But a puddle had gathered at my lip. He slipped and fell and cracked open his head. I stayed upright. I felt pity for him but not sadness, because he was old and was going to die anyway. The next day his sister found him. She sold me in a yard sale that spring for five dollars.

When I was a bowl I was force-fed the most revolting food. I became weary of being handled and was almost grateful when the oaf threw me against the wall. He wasn't angry with me; my death was incidental to something that neither of us can remember.

The last I remember I belonged to a girl who insisted I call her W. I humored her games. She may have been my favorite owner. She kept me in her pocket and held me when she was scared. I may have been a rock or a precious stone. I couldn't see myself, because she always kept me in her pocket. But I was dense and heavy and probably black, obsidian even. She told me that the universe had deceived her, and she had been born unintentionally. It had been a mistake. What she wanted more than anything was to return to her planet. Everyone there was named W, which is why she wanted me to call her that. I don't know if she ever made it back. Once she was locked in a room and used me to break a windowpane so that she could escape.

Now I'm trying to figure out what I am. Someone comes every day and holds me down while pouring sour liquid down my throat. I am forced to speak, though I have nothing to say. Their faces come close to mine, and they say I am like them, but I am not. I vomit on their sleeves and scream, but they don't understand.

The Secret of Chloe the Dog

Nancy Drew, an attractive girl of eighteen, was driving home along a country road in her new dark-blue convertible. She had just delivered some legal papers for her father. Now she had some business of her own.

It was sweet of Dad to give me this car for my birthday, she thought. And it's fun to help him in his work.

Nancy possessed no outstanding talents or traits, other than her hair, which, it could not be denied, gleamed more than ordinary hair. It was voluminous, as well. She was certainly well-groomed. Aside from her hair, she was plump from lack of exercise and sometimes out-and-out laziness. Her schoolwork was subpar, her athletic abilities yawn-inducing, and when she spoke, she did so with a lisp not because of a natural defect, which would have been understandable, but because of her inability to see why it mattered.

Her father, a well-known lawyer in their home town of River Heights, often discussed puzzling aspects of cases with his blonde, blue-eyed daughter in the hope that his work might spark her intellect and spur her on to greater things. He was constantly thinking of ways to get Nancy off his hands. He wanted to retire soon and move to Barcelona. But he couldn't take the girl with him. She would be a drag on his life, and his libido.

Smiling, Nancy said to herself, "Dad depends on my intuition."

The car sped along River Road until it came to an intersection.

"Oh, I forget which way to turn!"

She had left the directions in her coat pocket back home. It was unbelievably distressing to her to make a decision like this. She turned the nose of the car right, then left again, and finally drove the car around in a circle. Eventually a police officer noticed her indecision and pulled over to help her.

"Looks like you're lost," he said, tipping his hat forward, so that it almost fell into Nancy's lap.

"Oh! I forget which way to go!" Nancy said, balling her hands into tight little fists and punching the steering wheel.

"Depends on where you want to go."

Nancy noticed how handsome the officer was. She smiled, then covered her mouth with her hand, because she did not want to appear too forward.

"I'm looking for clues," she said softly. "I want to solve a mystery for Dad."

"That's pretty vague." The officer smiled back at her.

"It's just that…Oh, you'll think it's stupid."

"Try me." The officer was clearly enjoying this. His head was completely inside the car now, so that if Nancy had rolled up the window, she could have beheaded him. Instead, she kissed him on the mouth.

"Have I done anything wrong?" Nancy smirked.

He opened Nancy's car door and asked her to step out.

"I'm haunted," she said and put one hand over her eyes to shield them from the sun.

"Hunted?" His face was close to hers now, and he was rubbing himself against her yellow dress. "I'll keep you safe. Who's the guy? I'll find him."

Nancy said nothing but stood with her bodice gaping open. One of her breasts had popped out of her bra. The nipple turned upward to an astounding degree, like the finger of a medieval saint pointing toward heaven. She wore a special bra and performed exercises to achieve this effect.

"C'mon, let's go down the side," he said, indicating with a nod the desired embankment.

"It does look soft." Nancy giggled. She walked around to the other side of the car and looked down. Green, feathery grass grew along the embankment. It moved a little in the wind. The officer came up from behind and playfully pushed her. She somersaulted forward and landed on her back.

"Wheeee!" she said.

The officer leapt to her side.

When she awoke at noon, the officer was gone. Nancy felt unbelievably sensual lying in the sun, her dress torn open, her underwear tossed aside, her body sweaty and beginning to sunburn. Her nipples felt raw.

He left me here—all alone! she thought frantically. Anyone could have come along and done anything to me! She huffed. Then she smiled and yawned and gathered her things and dressed herself. Her purse was hanging from the branch of a nearby tree. Inside was a note.

> I know about your mystery now, Nance. There's a farmhouse about a mile from here. Go there, but don't tell them I sent you. Say you're an interior designer and call yourself Stacey.
> Take Care, Officer Rowlandson

"Stacey! What an awful name!" Nancy walked slowly up the embankment with her arms at her sides. It was more exercise than she had had in a long time, and she was beginning to get winded. Her convertible was where she had left it, everything in its proper place, the heirloom blanket still in the back seat, the metal box where she kept her expensive jewelry, and even the keys dangling from the ignition.

All was well, except—

Nancy gasped.

Someone had keyed her brand new convertible!

She had to step back to read the words: "Die Bitch!"

"Who would do such a terrible thing?"

Nancy looked around. Across the road, three Mexican men were loading crates of corn into a truck. Nancy ran over to them, waving her arms.

"Did you see who did that to my car?"

They looked at each other and laughed.

"My car! C-A-R. Caaaaar." she said. Nancy tried desperately to remember what she had learned in Spanish class. What was the word for car? Or scoundrels?

"*¡Cojones!*" she yelled. "*¡Muchos diablos!*"

The men doubled over with laughter. Their faces turned completely red. One of them tipped over in the grass.

"Drunks! Stupid drunks!" she yelled. "I know an officer, you know. We're very close friends."

The men stopped laughing not because they were scared of Nancy's threats but because the joke had run its course, and they wanted to get her off their hands.

"It was the officer that did it, miss," one of them said, the shortest. He took his baseball cap off his head and wiped the sweat away with the back of his hand. "The officer messed with your car."

"The Peeeegs!" the taller one yelled. He made little oinking noises as he threw crates into the truck.

"I don't know nothing more," the first man said. "But he went that way."

He pointed down River Road, toward the mountains.

"*Gracias*," Nancy said, her eyes lowered. She thought it meant something else, and she was too disheartened to think of the right words.

Nancy didn't know what to think. Should she go to the farmhouse as Officer Rowlandson said? Or drive in the opposite direction where the Mexican man pointed? First, she would drive home and talk to her father.

Carson Drew owned a palatial estate in the heart of River Heights. From the top floor, he could survey the entire valley and even make out the skyline of the nearest city. But he didn't live on the top floor, or even the second or first. He lived in a little room in the basement and rarely left, except for business. But most of the time he sent Nancy out into the world to do his bidding for him.

"Nipples were raw, you said?" Carson Drew said, after Nancy told him about the events of the day. She kept no secrets from her father. It was a habit of hers, important for solving mysteries, that carried over into the rest of her life.

"It felt good at first," Nancy said. "And then it felt terrible, and then when I saw what happened with the car and what those Mexicans told me!" Nancy leaned against a stack of legal documents as she spoke. Her father's office was filled with paper and filing cabinets. She could hardly make out his face and body. She only saw two eyes and a mouth. It seemed like his appendages were made out of paper.

"You can't trust foreigners," Carson Drew said. "If it were up to me, I'd have them all deported."

"You think they lied to me?"

"Of course they lied to you, and it was probably those bozos who vandalized your car."

"Played a trick on me," Nancy sulked.

"That's right, dear."

"And right when I was hot on the trail." Her cheeks flushed with rage.

"It happens to the best of us. You'll learn, as you gain experience, who to trust and who's a born liar."

"I feel so foolish, Dad."

"Now, don't get down on yourself. Listen, I have a friend who owns an auto shop. It's just beyond the farmhouse that Officer Rowlandson told you to go to. Follow out his orders, and then stop at the auto shop on the way back. By the end of the day, you'll be back on the right track, and the car will be fixed up."

"Oh, Dad! I'm so glad I came home!"

Nancy crawled over the desk and kissed her father on the cheek. As she was slipping out the door, Carson Drew said: "Oh just one thing, Nancy. Your little tryst with Rowlandson?"

Nancy raised an eyebrow.

"Let's just keep that between the two of us, shall we?"

"You bet, Dad."

It was almost two o'clock by the time Nancy reached the farmhouse. It wasn't a real working farm, none of the farms in River Heights were anymore. Instead it was a restored farmhouse with updated additions. The owners must be rich and stylish, "rural chic," Nancy thought. A chandelier hung from the porch and below that two older women were sitting on white wicker chairs with big, plush, grey cushions. The tables looked like they were made out of steel. A big white poodle sat at their feet.

Oh, I hate poodles! Nancy thought as she pulled into the driveway. But then she remembered that her name was Stacey, and she was an interior designer, not the daughter of an important lawyer in town. Stacey probably liked poodles.

"I will have to lie," Nancy said. "For the sake of truth."

When she approached the porch, the dog jumped up, ran over to her, and pawed at her dress.

"Chloe!" one of the women shouted. "Chloe, no!"

The dog leapt up and slammed its paws down on Nancy's shoulders, knocking her to the ground. The dog was enormous, at least twice Nancy's size. It straddled her crumpled body, its front paws on either side of her face, like a vice grip. Drool gathered in Chloe's lips and then dripped onto Nancy's face, washing her lipstick away.

"Oh, it's no trouble!" Nancy cried. "I love dogs!"

"Chloe, leave it! Leave it, Chloe!"

The two women came running. It took both of them to pull the dog off Nancy.

Her dress was ripped open for the second time that day. She caught her image in the reflection of the car window. I look amazing and tragic, she thought. No matter how hard she tried to get that tousled look, only sex and trauma made her hair look like that. Her breasts had once again popped out of her bra.

"Oh, dear! Look what Chloe has done!" The two women took hold of Nancy and buttoned up the front of her dress. They took her by the hand and led her to the porch.

"I'm sorry. She's a vicious animal. Aren't you Chloe?" Chloe sat in the shade of the porch like a sphinx. Her black eyes remained unmoved. Her poodle ears hung down on both sides of her face like a big winter hat. She looked straight ahead, contemplating the empty air.

"She fatally wounded a child, one of our neighbors. And now the courts say we have to put her down. But she can be a gentle creature, too. We love her."

"It must be hard for you," Nancy said, "to have a dog like that."

"Yes, it is. Our nephew's coming later today to shoot her."

"Your nephew? Is he a trained animal killer?" Nancy asked.

"No, not that. He's a police officer. He shoots criminals, not animals, but the technique is the same."

"I just realized we haven't introduced ourselves. How rude! I'm Eveline, and this is my partner, Joyce. I assume you are Stacey from River Heights Design?"

Nancy tried to keep her cool but her mind was racing. A police officer? Were these Officer Rowlandson's aunts?

I would have worn a better dress, Nancy thought.

"Do you have anything to drink?" she asked. "It's so hot today, and I'm thirsty."

Eveline shot out of her seat. "We have ice tea! I'll be right back."

That bought Nancy some time, so she could regain her composure.

"I am Stacey," she said. It came out stiffly, and she couldn't think of anything else to say. It was impossible to think of herself as a Stacey or what a Stacey might say or think. All she could think about was Officer Rowlandson and whether these women, Eveline and Joyce, were his aunts.

Joyce said, "We thought so."

Nancy smiled and looked around.

"Did you bring the swatches?"

Darn! Why didn't she think this through before she came? Of course an interior designer would have swatches and other things, like paint chips and sketches.

"I had them," Nancy stammered. "But Chloe knocked them out of my hand when she attacked me. Look, I'm bleeding."

She pointed to a trickle of blood on her ankle.

"I'll get the first aid kit," Joyce said.

That was quick thinking, Nancy thought. She put her hands behind her head and leaned back in her wicker seat, beaming with pride.

After a while, Nancy realized she had fallen asleep. Where were Joyce and Eveline? Chloe was in the exact same position, fixated on nothingness.

Nancy walked over to the dog.

"Do you know you're going to die?" she said with a pout.

She reached out and scratched behind one of Chloe's ears. Chloe remained unmoved.

"I just hope Officer Rowlandson is professional and trained. No need for an animal to suffer unnecessarily."

Chloe yawned and put her head in between her paws.

Nancy decided to go inside the farmhouse. If Joyce and Eveline caught her, she would say that she wanted to get a sense of the layout. They had hired her, after all, to decorate their house.

To Nancy's surprise, the inside of the house was already comfortably furnished. It was decked out with new furniture, new curtains, everything freshly painted, and framed pictures on the walls. A grey, even light permeated the entire house. Nancy walked around the first floor, picking things up and setting them back down. Everything appeared to have been bought that morning. It looked like a showroom, not a house that anyone actually lived in. Maybe they had a carriage house that needed to be decorated? It didn't make any sense.

Nancy returned to the front stairwell and tiptoed up the stairs. They hired me to come here, she thought. I'm not doing anything wrong or out of the ordinary. And my name is Stacey.

When she reached the top, she could hear Eveline and Joyce whispering in one of the bedrooms. At least she thought it was them. The murmuring came and went like a breeze in and out of a window. The upstairs was also suffused with a grey, even light, and everything was freshly painted.

What is she doing here? Nancy thought she heard Eveline say.

"How did she find us?" Joyce replied in a placid voice. But beneath that, Nancy could hear the panic in her voice.

"Knock, knock, it's Stacey," Nancy said softly at the door.

"Oh, Stacey!" Eveline exclaimed. "We're sorry to leave you down there all alone with Chloe."

"We've just received a terrible phone call," Joyce said. "And it's put us in no mood for company."

"What happened?" Nancy asked. "If you don't mind my asking?"

"It's our lawyer," Joyce said with great seriousness.

"He's a crook," Eveline said.

"How do you know?" Nancy said. "Did he call you?"

"Of course not," Joyce said. "He never would look us in the eye, and now we know why."

"What has he done?" Nancy gasped.

"Taken all our money, that's what, and left town! He left for Barcelona this morning with that fat, spoiled daughter of his."

Nancy began to shake. The light coming through the window was beginning to fade, and the faces of Eveline and Joyce went dark. She could only see their lips moving, but couldn't hear the words. A shadow fell across the bed. The two women sat on either side.

"What was his name?" Nancy whispered.

"His name?" Joyce seemed confused.

"Your lawyer?"

"Only the most respectable lawyer in town," Eveline spit out the words. "Carson Drew!"

Nancy thought she might strike her face.

Nancy ran out of the room and down the stairs. When she reached the bottom, she thought she could hear laughter coming from the bedroom, but it could have been anything.

"This is no time for paranoia, Nancy. You've got to keep your head."

Once she reached her convertible, she debated what to do. It couldn't be her father getting on a plane with her, Nancy, by his side, headed for Barcelona with a suitcase of cash he had stolen from two women? This was insanity. Eveline and Joyce were as insane as that horrible dog, and that was all there was to it.

Her immediate desire was to go straight home and talk to her father, to clear things up right away. But that would have seemed suspicious. Didn't he tell her to go to the auto shop to get her car fixed up after going to the farmhouse? If she didn't do that first, he might think she didn't trust him and rejected his favors, when he had never been anything but kind to Nancy, always sending her out on adventures and buying her a convertible to ride in style and even, when she got herself into a jam, like she did earlier today, giving her the name of a reputable auto shop where they would fix her up right away.

First, I'll go to the auto shop, Nancy thought. And then straight home!

The auto shop wasn't nearly as close as her father had said it would be. She drove and drove, and by the time she saw the sign for Riverside Auto Repair the sun had dipped below the mountains.

They might not even be open, she thought, as she pulled up to the garage. She got out of the car and looked around a little. It seemed completely deserted. She thought it must be closed, but she rang the bell anyway, just to be sure.

A man dressed in blue coveralls came around the corner.

"Officer Rowlandson!" Nancy cried. "You work here!"

"Shhhh. Keep your voice down."

"I'm sorry," Nancy said. "It's just that I was so surprised." He was wiping his tanned, muscular hands on a white towel. He did this quickly, then tossed the towel in a large cardboard box full of dirty towels.

"Police force doesn't pay what it used to. So I work here part-time. But I don't want anyone to know."

"That you're an officer?"

"Yes. Criminals don't respect you if they know you have a night job. They laugh in your face. They'll toss aside a loaded gun like it's a toy."

"I understand," Nancy said. "Am I the only one who knows?"

Officer Rowlandson didn't answer.

"I'm not in the mood for games, Stacey. Have you got some car trouble, or did you just come here to flirt with me?"

Nancy laughed. Stacey. She could play that game.

"And what's your name. Ray?"

"Yeah, actually. C'mon, Stacey, don't be an idiot. I don't want to play your games."

Nancy was shocked, but also excited. She decided to play along.

"I've been all over God's green Earth, Ray, chasing your mysteries. I've been to the farmhouse and met your aunts and was attacked by that poodle, and they said the most horrible things about my father and about me. And I would have driven straight home, but something told me to come here, and now I know why, Ray. It was you who vandalized my car, wasn't it?"

Ray smiled. "You really take things to heart, don't you Stacey? And you watch too many movies. Ok, my boss is gone."

Ray grabbed Nancy by the waist and threw her down on the dirty rags. His hands were strong and nimble, first from shooting criminals and then from fixing cars.

Nancy's breasts were bigger than before. Her hair felt rough in his hands. He thrust a hand into her underwear, like before, but this time it felt different. She felt like a different person.

"Harder, Ray. Oh that feels good."

"Stacey, you dirty girl…"

Afterward, when they were dressing, Nancy said in a tone of great seriousness:

"I've found it, Ray, I've found it. I'm glad I didn't give up the search."

"Whatever you say, Stacey. Let's take a look at your car."

The car was not the same. It was not a dark-blue convertible but a dingy brown sedan.

"Where's my beautiful car?" she asked.

"Stacey, enough already. I want to go home."

"And stop calling me that!" Nancy almost screamed. "I thought we were slumming it!"

"Whatever you say. I'm outta here."

Ray walked around to the side of the building where his police motorcycle was waiting. He hopped on the back of it and drove away.

"Serve and protect, you bastard!" Nancy could hardly believe the words that were coming out of her mouth. She looked at herself in the driver's side window. Her hair was frizzy; her face looked ugly and damaged.

"I look like white trash," she said with disgust.

There was only one thing to do now. Go see her father.

Nancy drove in a rage, and when she reached the gates of her home, she was aghast. The exterior code would not work. She parked the car a few blocks down. So as not to raise the suspicions of the neighbors, she thought. And then immediately: What am I thinking? These are MY neighbors. I am Nancy Drew.

She walked two blocks and entered through a side gate. She went up to the house and looked through the window of her father's office. All the lights were out. She couldn't see inside. She tried all the doors, but they were locked. The mailbox was full of mail. It hadn't been picked up in weeks. She thought about breaking a window, but then the police would come. Maybe Officer Rowlandson would come. Could she trust him? Probably not. She felt despondent. Why had he abandoned her like this? What was Carson Drew thinking?

Then a light went on next-door, and another light. She saw men moving in the bushes. One said into his walkie-talkie: "That's her, all right."

Nancy ran and ran, as fast and as hard as she could. She had never worked this hard in her life. She felt like a hunted animal.

I thought it was all fun and games, she thought, and, for the first time, she was struck by the stupidity of her thoughts and the futility of all her vain pursuits. Her father was a criminal, and had sold her out in the worst possible way, and she knew it all along but didn't want to see it.

I've been a fool! she thought.

Nancy drove straight to the farmhouse. It was the only place to go. Eveline and Joyce came to the door in their nightgowns.

"Oh, you've come at last!" Eveline said.

"God bless you, Stacey," Joyce said.

"Pay me first," Nancy said. "I've got no time for games."

Eveline went back inside the house and came back with an envelope.

"Five hundred dollars, just as we agreed on the phone."

Nancy counted out the bills.

"It's short. Only four-eighty," she said, annoyed.

Eveline and Nancy waited outside, while Joyce went back into the house to find another bill.

"We thought you'd be here earlier," Eveline said.

"I had some things I had to do," Nancy said.

"Well, we are enormously grateful to you."

"Don't be," Nancy said. "It's just a job."

Then Joyce came out of the house. The three of them walked to a shed in the backyard, next to a big weeping willow. Joyce held the gun.

"Should we say a prayer?" Joyce said.

"If you want," Nancy said.

"I can't think of anything."

"No one ever can."

They brought the dog out on a leash. Chloe had that same placid look, expressing neither anxiety nor hope. It came forward and bowed its head.

"Do it now," Eveline said.

"I can't bear to look," Joyce said. She handed the gun to Nancy, who pressed it to the dog's temple and pulled the trigger.

Brains splattered on the white nightgowns of Joyce and Eveline. But somehow Nancy came out clean.

Amusement Park

Barbara told me this story.

Several years ago, Barbara, along with her sister and her sister's boyfriend, took a trip to an amusement park in central Ohio. They were all excited that afternoon, because they had not spent time together in quite a while, and, on top of that, it was recently announced that the sister and her boyfriend, Tim, were getting married in the spring. Tim, in celebration, decided to pay for everyone's admission, which amounted to thirty dollars. Everyone was having a great time; Tim and Barbara shared some cotton candy, and the sister sat on a bench feeding birds while the two of them went on the roller coasters, which she did not like.

That day, after lunch, while Tim and Barbara were riding the Orient Express, the sister witnessed an unusual spectacle. Two friends, one fat and one skinny, were taking turns climbing into a small opening in the center of the roller coaster's spiral so that when the coaster came around the track it would pass first on the right of the man, then on the left, then again on the right, quickly around the spiral, but the man in the center would be left unharmed.

The two friends did this, one at a time, three or four times, but on the fifth time, as the skinny man nestled himself into the spiral alcove and just as the roller coaster was approaching, the fat man jumped on top of his friend. Both were horribly maimed. But the story does not end there. Barbara's sister passed out from the shock and was immediately rushed to the hospital. Here it was discovered that, because of the depth of her attention to the tragedy, track marks from the rollercoaster actually appeared on her body, piercing the skin and muscle and nearly shattering the bone.

This affected Barbara as well, because she and her sister were close, but she was actually more disturbed by what followed. Later, after her sister was recovering in the intensive care unit, and Barbara was keeping an all-night vigil in the waiting room, she happened to overhear two nurses chatting in that perfunctory way, as Barbara said, the way that people do when they are on intimate terms with pain.

"If only she," said one of the nurses, referring to the sister, "could distance herself, like the rest of us, she would not suffer so much."

"Or laugh a little, not be so serious," said the other nurse while peering into a microscope.

Later that night, Barbara had a dream in which she peered not into a microscope but a hole in the center of her sister's head. Inside she saw a smaller version of her sister, diminished, but still alive, potting a few plants.

Letter from Rosaline

I HAVE JUST RECEIVED A LETTER in the mail from my friend Rosaline, who works at the same company as me.

She had gone out for the evening to a movie and, at a certain point toward the end of the film, she had the distinct feeling that a man was reaching into her purse.

She felt in the dark under the seat where her purse was stowed away, the soft leather of the purse and then the soft flesh of a hand, but when she screamed and jumped to her feet and spun around in the darkness, there was no one behind her, no one to the side of her, except for her friend, whose popcorn flew in all directions.

Someone shouted, "Sit down!" and so she did.

But the story does not end there. Later, when she arrived home, things were not right. The flowerpot that normally concealed her house key was overturned and also smashed into bits; the doormat was not in its usual spot in front of the door but pushed off to one side and upside down.

She reached into her purse to see if the hand was there, but it was not there. Someone had been in her house instead.

She reached for the knob, but the door was locked and the key was gone, so she had to call a locksmith to get back into the apartment.

The locksmith did not come for several hours, and when he did, he popped the door open in an instant and began a triumphant procession through the apartment. Rosaline suffered through this performance while sitting on a stool in the middle of the living room.

That night she dreamed that she and the locksmith were cleaning the rugs of an enormous cathedral, dragging each rug by hand to the vestibule, cleaning them, then moving them back into place.

Rosaline wondered, as she held the rug in one hand and gazed off in the direction of the altar, whether it was the locksmith's hand in her purse, whether the locksmith had also invaded her apartment, and whether he would now reveal his true identity to her.

He did not.

Instead, Rosaline awoke in her own apartment. The thief or thieves had not stolen anything and had kindly deposited the key in her mailbox, which she found the next day.

Besides the broken flowerpot, Rosaline had suffered no material loss and closed her letter by saying, "People say it is horrible to think of a stranger being in your house, but actually I feel exceptionally safe."

MAG

SHE CAN'T REMEMBER THE NIGHT AT THE PARTY. There aren't any windows in this room. She can't tell what time of day it is. The desk light is still on. The room is neat and clean. The walls are painted maroon, not a color she would choose. It's not her room; this is not her house. The sheets are expensive. They feel soft on her skin. She realizes, with surprise, that it's not just the sheets that are soft. Someone has shaved her legs and, also, she realizes, her head. On the pillow next to her is a clear plastic bag filled with her hair. It is full—she had long, thick hair—and is tied at the top with a tag that says, somewhat unnecessarily, "Your Hair." She reaches up to feel the shape of her exposed head, then her face, and discovers, to her relief, that her eyebrows are still there. Her eyes, naturally. Also her mouth. Some things cannot be taken, she thinks, and this thought brings some relief. Wigs are so lifelike these days. No one would know the difference. That was the important thing. She walks to the desk with the sheet wrapped around her like a toga. Above the desk is a dark, greasy square where the mirror should be. The drawers are locked. The light can't be turned off. It has no switch. The door is also locked. There's nothing else in the room. She gets back into bed. Soon she is asleep.

He floats down the lazy river. The water is clear and aquamarine. He can see all the way to the bottom and also far ahead of him and behind. He is a handsome man and also rich. He can have whatever woman he wants. But he wanted her, and she did something very bad, and now he has punished her. I trusted her, he thinks, and she betrayed me in the worst possible way. And she left something disgusting in the dishwasher. The floaties are white, puffy clouds, softer than any mattress. He reclines back on his floatie and stares into the sun. It's a hot, cloudless day in the desert. Everyone is enjoying the water park. My water park, he thinks with satisfaction. His body is tan and lean. He enjoys his body almost but not quite as much as he enjoys hers. But it requires discipline. Especially for her. Things can deteriorate quickly if you're not careful. It takes a lot of work to be beautiful. There's a summer buzz in the air, the insects are alive, and those sounds mix with the nearby generator that powers the lazy river. It's all humming. He likes his body to be hot but his extremities to be cool. He lets his feet and the tips of his fingers graze the surface of the water. He thinks of an iceberg floating on a clear blue ocean. The iceberg stops. People are talking. He sits up. The lazy river has stopped. The water is still. He sees a man ahead of him sit up and look around. His skin is grey and hairless. He is bald. The rich, handsome man shakes with fear. His mouth fills up with saliva, and he turns to spit into the water. Mixed with the saliva is a little drop of blood. It contaminates the river, and the man nearly vomits. He has to choke it down. Is that him? It couldn't be. It couldn't be. God no. But he knows that it *is* him, that it *must* be him. On the back of the grey man's head is a tattoo that he recognizes. It says, "MAG" in big, black stenciled letters. I'm finished, he thinks. He looks down. He has an erection. That's how he knows. That's how he knows he's finished.

The door opens. He walks in and sits on the edge of the bed. She has already heard him but does not turn over. He gives her rump a shake, says, "Wake up sweetie." She says, "Don't call me that. You don't even know me." He says that's true, that he doesn't know her. "Where am I?" she asks. "Are we in your house?" He says that's unimportant. He has some questions for her about the party, about the night before. "I trusted you," he says. "I can't remember what happened," she says, which is true. "What happened?" she asks earnestly. He looks at her suspiciously at first, but then he can see she is telling the truth. "You've done something terrible," he says, and the thing is so terrible he cannot say it aloud. That is also why he has put her in this room and removed the mirror and left the light on. "Did you shave my head?" she asks. "No," he says. "No, I did not."

He paddles to the edge of the lazy river and lifts himself onto the shore. Water streams off his back and down his sides. The concrete burns his feet. His wet parts dry immediately. He still has an erection, but it's fading. He walks as fast as he can to the bathhouse. Inside it is cool and pungent with body smells:

piss and shit and sweat, but not blood. It smells like the reptile house at the zoo: filthy but bloodless. He opens a stall and stands with his shins touching the rim of the toilet. He thinks of her with kindness now, and real affection, because he thinks this will alleviate his fear. Three or four boys run past the stall, their wet feet slapping the concrete. Bam! Bam! Bam! One of them pounds the stall. Then everything goes quiet. He stands on the rim of the toilet and crouches down to hide. He watches the grey feet walk past, watches them enter the stall next to him. The sound of his grey piss hitting the water. He waits there until the grey man is gone, then he runs as far and as fast as he can, out into the sun, away from here, away from the grey man, his skin burning.

"I am the owner of this house," he says, "and everything in it belongs to me. And everything that takes place in it is my concern." She says she understands and tries to explain to him that bad people came and undermined her authority and did bad things, because they knew they could get away with it. He doesn't believe her. He continues talking and as he talks he slides his hand along her shin. Whoever shaved her legs did careful work and used a fresh blade. Her skin shines. He says there's something she can do to make up for it, a little bit, a little bit at a time. "Not now," she says. "Come back later, and bring me something to eat."

The rich, handsome man drives home, first speeding, but then slower, because this would be a terrible time to get pulled over. His feet are bare on the pedals. He forgot his shoes at the water park. There's something crawling across his foot, but he doesn't dare look at it. It's making a buzzing sound. He drives across the desert through several mirages. It's the middle of July, and everything's on fire. They keep sending the national guard up into the hills to put out the fires, and no one's supposed to water their lawns. When he arrives home, the gate is ajar. Carlos is watering the lawn with his crew. The man reaches down and touches the thing on his foot. It's a locust. He flicks it into the gravel. Then he crushes it with his heel. "What are you doing?" he yells to Carlos. Carlos looks up through a spray of water, shimmering and rainbow-colored. He says something in Spanish to his crew. The arc of water from his hose rises for a moment, then deflates and finally dies. The last few trickles land on the locust. It isn't dead, but its wing is broken. He hops away. The man goes into the house and bellows something, a woman's name. A woman dressed for golf comes to the edge of the upper-floor landing. He tells her to pack her things, that they need to leave town. "I'm not going anywhere," she says.

The owner of the house returns with a tray of food. "I made it myself," he says. "My housekeeper left after she saw the mess you made." The shaved woman smiles and pulls the sheet up around her armpits as she sits up. On the tray is an assortment of crudités. She doesn't recognize the food but doesn't say so. She doesn't want the owner to know how unsophisticated she is. She picks up what looks like a tiny fried octopus, but he takes it out of her hand. "Not so fast," he says. He places it back on the tray next to a pile of berries and a saucer filled with an orange sauce. "I want you to tell me what happened last night," he says, "and each time you tell me something true, I will give you a bite of food." "I don't like this game," she says, crossing her arms and leaning back against the headboard. She pouts a little and, at the same time, lets the sheet fall, so he can see the tops of her breasts. He wonders how old she is. "How do you know? You've never played it before." "I've played it before," she says. "My brother and I used to play that game when we were little. We never had enough food in the house, and it made what we had last longer." The owner smiles. It's a gentle smile. He likes thinking of the shaved woman as a young girl, which must not have been very long ago. She has a sweetness to her, even if time and circumstance have forced her to do bad things against her will. "Well, you've never played it with me," he says.

The woman can say what she wants because the staircase is torn away. She comes to the edge of the makeshift bannister made out of bare lumber slapped together with nails. She tells him that he's a world-class a-hole and that wherever he's going he can go by himself. She's dressed smartly, in her golf apparel, and as she says this she pretends to tee off. The workmen cease hammering and look up to see how he'll respond. He runs toward the back staircase, which is still intact, across the ripped up carpet and piles of sawdust, and steps on a nail. He screams in agony and falls on his side. The woman laughs and walks away. She's not that cruel. She thinks he is faking it. The workmen run over. One of them says, "Call an ambulance," but the rich, handsome man says, "No, no don't do that. I've got a plane to catch." He looks across the kitchen, or where the kitchen used to be. The wall is torn away. Plastic rattles around the edges. On the floor is a smashed sink and a burned-out spot where the oven used to be. Beyond that he can see the swimming desert, the red, swollen sun, and the hills on fire.

At first she can't remember anything, but then her hunger makes her remember. "I only invited three people," she says. "Three of my closest friends." He examines the corners of her mouth to see if she is telling the truth and decides that she is and hands her the fried octopus. "No," she says. "Dip it in the sauce." A little bit dribbles on the sheet. He hates that. He is, by nature, a neat man. "Go on," he says, wiping the sheet with a napkin while she talks. "Well they brought their friends, and I didn't want to turn them away. I was ready for a party, you know? I thought six isn't that much more than three, and nine isn't much more than six, and twelve isn't—you can see where this is going? It got out of hand pretty fast. I knew it was wrong, but I was having such a fabulous time, you know, and I don't get out enough. Everyone says that I spend too much time alone." She opens her mouth and closes her eyes. He places something green and slimy on her tongue, still alive, still moving. "Mmmm, salty," she says.

He doesn't pack anything. He can buy clothes when he gets there. He finds his passport, he finds his keys, he finds his gym shoes. Carlos hands him a blue dress shirt. "How did you find this?" he says. "We have a ladder," Carlos says. "I climbed it and found it in your closet." "Thank you," the rich, handsome man says. "The renovation is postponed until I get back. Tell everyone to go home and await my command." His voice is shaky and awkward and his phrasing archaic. He can't think straight. The nail wasn't old, but it wasn't new either. It might have had rust on it or bacteria. "We know," Carlos says, wiping his forehead with a handkerchief. "Someone came an hour ago and said the same thing. He told us you were coming. He said the same thing to us that you just said to me." His mouth moves, and a second later the words come out. "Who?" the rich, handsome man says. "Who came?" Carlos looks at his pal for confirmation. "A grey man," he says. "He said the renovations were done, that you wouldn't need the house no more. That you were going away." The rich, handsome man breaks out in a fresh sweat. The fever comes on fast. He can feel vomit inching its way up his throat and chokes it down once more.

"By that time the house was full. It couldn't be stopped. They kept coming and coming, like a plague. Some of their houses were in the hills, and the national guard evacuated them earlier in the day. They might all lose their homes. They didn't care. They were anarchic; the energy, it felt so real, so alive. I didn't want it to stop. I couldn't have stopped it even if I tried. It didn't matter who you were. Everyone was welcome. We stopped being people. We started being a swarm." "You were drugged," he says. "Someone brought drugs to my house." "No," she says. "I was sober; everyone was. It might have been the heat or the fires, but it wasn't that." He hands her a split carrot with a red vein running down the center. She takes it with her teeth and nips his finger playfully. "Someone suggested a game of charades. Have you played before?" She can see that he's jealous of the fun he missed, that he isn't often invited to parties, and when he is, he doesn't enjoy them very much. She touches his arm to reassure him, to make him feel included. "I was up first. I had to act out the French Revolution. Can you believe it? At first I pretended to be Napoleon. You know, with that hat? I made the shape with my hands, and then I remembered that was earlier. I felt like an idiot. I tried to undo it, but it just confused people. Then I remember that painting, the famous one?" "By Delacroix?" "Maybe him. I couldn't remember the name. I just remembered the painting from my high school history book. A boy with two pistols in his hands and angry men fighting for their freedom, dead men on the ground, some of them naked, and in the middle a woman holding the French flag. I remembered that part especially. I took off my shirt and held an invisible flag over my head, and everyone guessed easily." The owner of the house says, "Why don't you show me?" and she does, and he reaches out to touch her bare skin. "You're beautiful," he says.

He lets the workmen bandage his foot. They insist on it. Carlos says, "You must go to the hospital right away when you land," and the rich, handsome man promises him that he will. He is touched by this kindness and shakes Carlos's hand and says, "Have you ever been hunted my man?" and Carlos misunderstands him and says, "No, *señor*, not ever." He says men do the hunting, and women run. That's how it is in his world. He thinks his boss got into trouble with a lady friend. But it's not his place to give advice. He looks down for a second, and when he looks up again the rich, handsome man has hobbled halfway down the gravel driveway. Pretty fast for a man with a nail hole in his foot. But that's not his problem. By the time his crew has packed up, the rich, handsome man is already walking into the airport.

He wants to make love to her now. "I want you," he says. "I want you now." He's running his hands over her naked body and over her shaved head and kissing her mouth. "Don't you want to know how we destroyed your house? Don't you want to hear the rest of my story?" "No," he says. "I forgive you. I forgive everything," but she pushes him away and says firmly, "No. I want to finish my story. I want to tell you how it ends." He stops. He's not a rapist. He's not that kind of man. So he waits, though he makes his annoyance known. He doesn't like being toyed with either. The shaved woman makes a promise to him. "Once I'm done with the story, I'll do whatever you like." This pacifies him. He moves away from her. She covers herself with the sheet. She starts talking again, but he no longer cares about his house or her story. He's thinking of what he's going to do to her when she's done.

The airport is crowded. Everyone's leaving town. "The fires," the flight attendant says. "Everything's burning. Nothing can be done." "What's left?" the rich, handsome man says. "Where can I go?" "I told you," she says, shaking her head into the blinking computer screen. "You can't go anywhere. You're stuck." He screams and pounds the counter with his fist. His sweaty hair falls forward. His mouth fills up with spit. His foot throbs. It's infected, and the infection is working its way into his bloodstream and upward into his head. The flight attendant calls a guard over and the two converse for a minute, taking turns pointing at inexplicable blinking things on the screen. She says, "Is that?" and he says, "It may be, it may be," in a slow drawl that makes the rich, handsome man furious. Finally, the woman says to him, "Well, it's your lucky day. Computer hid this one from us." "What is it? What's left?" the rich, handsome man says in a croak. "It's the last flight," she says, and both she and the guard smile at him. "The last flight out of here."

"By then your house was so full no one could move. We were all shoulder to shoulder, or back to back, writhing against one another like worms in a wormhole. Everyone lost everything. Nothing was left. The national guard had given up. They said nothing could be done. A chant went up. Let it all burn, they said. Let it all burn. We were going to start over, start fresh, and it all started here in your house. Right under your nose. While you weren't looking. It was growing here like some diabolic yeast. At the party. At my party." She stops. He gives her a napkin and a plastic cup filled with a sparkling beverage. She sips from it. "It may be your party, but it's still my house," he says, taking the cup back from her, scolding her, like a nurse tending an ungrateful invalid. "That's right," she says. "It is your house. And someone must have known it—though I have no idea how—because in the next round of charades, I picked your name. Everyone laughed. They were playing a joke on me. You know how inimitable you are?" "That's what everyone says." The owner smiles. "But I've never had any trouble playing myself." "Everyone was looking at me. Everyone was waiting to see what I would do." "What did you do?" he asks, leaning in. "This!" she says, with excitement. She makes a face, and it is exactly his face, and she makes a gesture with her hands, under the sheets. He can only see the outline of the gesture, but he recognizes it as his own. He is stunned. It is exactly the right thing. It is exactly the right thing to do.

The handsome, rich man walks for a long time to the terminal. It is so far away. And so difficult to walk. His foot has swollen to twice its size. He kicks the shoe away and walks on the bandaged foot. He walks down one corridor after another. The crowd thins out. It's only airport workers now, shutting down their kiosks for the day, mopping up. He stops to get a drink of water at the water fountain. His lips are dry and beginning to crack. The fever is burning him up. The nail must have been rusty. It doesn't matter. What matters is leaving, getting away from the grey man, getting away from MAG. When he reaches the terminal, it is empty, the lights are dim, no one is there to take his ticket. Doesn't matter, he thinks. The only thing that matters is getting on that plane. A hand appears with coral-colored nails. Attached to a woman, he assumes. The hand speaks. Points at the doorway. "No luggage," he says. "I'm traveling light." He walks down the ramp and lunges into the plane, as if it were a boat about to float away from the dock. Another set of hands helps him to his seat and straps him into place. He sits. He waits. He closes his eyes. He's made it. He's free.

"Then we reached the final round. Everyone wondered how it would end, what would be the last thing. It was my turn again. I took the slip of paper, opened it." The shaved woman stops. Her lips tremble. A terrified expression flashes across her face. "What was it? What did it say?" he asks, not because he's very interested, but because he wants her to finish so he can make love to her. "It said MAG," she says. And now she remembers, remembers how it felt to be at the party and how the mood became murderous. It moved through the crowd, emanating from no one. It was a possession that came from everyone at once. "What is that?" the owner asks impatiently. "What's MAG?" "MAG isn't anything," she says. "That's why I couldn't act it out. I didn't know what to do. I stood there, and everyone looked at me, but there was nothing I could do. It was impossible." She pauses. The owner looks at her. He thinks she is older than he thought at first. She must be nineteen, at least. No need to worry about parents coming round, making accusations. He moves toward her, puts his hands on her thighs. "Is that it?" he asks. "Is that the end?" "MAG isn't a person," she says, ignoring his question. "It's a thing that comes back when it's ignored, a grey thing, and everyone can see it, but they try to ignore it until they can't anymore." She takes one of his hands and plays with it. "It lives in the desert and takes possession of its inhabitants and settles its scores, whatever those happen to be." His face is close to hers now, and he's running his hand over her head. "How did you lose your hair?" he asks. "You look so pretty like this, and I can imagine you with any hair I like." "They shaved me," she says. "Or we shaved each other, I should say. Someone passed around razor blades. Your floor—you should have seen it—covered with hair like that. Then we smashed your furniture and burned everything in the backyard. I'm sorry. I know you hired me to house sit. And what a mess we made." She smiles. "Thank you for saving my hair," she says and sets her palm on top of the bag. "What about here?" he asks, putting his hand in between her legs. "I told you," she says. "They shaved everything."

In the plane, he can hear other passengers boarding, but he doesn't bother to open his eyes. It's of no concern to him.

"Are you done?" he says, his breath heavy now. It's getting hot in the room. He's sweating. "Yes," she says. "I'm done."

That buzz isn't the fuselage. It's locusts gathering on the wing.

She takes off his shirt and kisses his chest. He isn't a handsome man, but he's been a good listener, and that counts for something. She takes off his pants and climbs on top of him. He lets out a little moan when she pulls him inside of her. He says he's never had it this good. She takes a cherry tomato from the tray and pops it into his mouth. "I think you're telling the truth," she says.

The fires move down from the hills, across the desert, and into the cities. Nothing can be done.

THE BEARS AT BEDTIME

AT THE END OF YOUR TRAVELS, YOU DISCOVER a colony of
bears, and when you walk through the door, they let the con-
fetti fly. They love you and are soft and warm, and they give you
soft pets and comfort you when you are scared. One is playing
the harp and another the mandolin. They love to hear their
music—not out of vanity but because they love to hear it—and
to see faces soften and hearts soften when they play it.

Some of them have soft curls, and others have silky fur,
and they don't mind if you touch them when they play their
instruments. A couple of smaller bears each take you by the
hand and look up at you and smile. They tell you a story about
a string that lost its way in the forest but eventually found its
way home and was taken and knit into a sweater. A soft light
falls from the sky and through the windows of the cathedral,

warming your face and chest. The bears cheer. They are not cheering for you exactly, but you are part of it, maybe even a big part.

You let your body slacken and fall and are caught, always. Someone or something is always there, always there to catch you: a fertile emptiness. Even when it feels like nothing is there, something is, and it's made of pure softness and beneath that, a bare wood floor, very flat and stable, extremely well-constructed, that holds it all up. You can lie down on it with all the bears and be comfortable and know that you will not rise or fall in the night but be perfectly even through all your dreams and nightmares. It's fine to feel whatever you feel; the bears have felt it all before and are not bothered or thrown off their tune by it.

They close all the shutters and turn off the lights, or dim them rather, so there's a soft haze of warm yellow light in the cathedral. There are other people, but almost everyone's asleep or preoccupied with their mental objects, fuzzy around the edges, though the center is clear. The bears know they're not real or at least not to be taken literally. There is only softness and inwardness and warm cider for these bears. That's all they know and all they take seriously. The rest is of a piece with vanity, lost causes, and desperate grasping. They try not to be judgmental but can't help but dismiss the delusions and vanities of people. They distract them, or try to, with their own brand of softness and play and take away the sharp edges so everyone can romp and not cut themselves. And they have a good work ethic for creatures so bent on softness and relaxation but are not above taking a nap in the middle of the day if that needs to happen. They let the humans sleep for as long as they like and always treat them with kindness, though they laugh at their stupidity.

Sometimes they clap but so softly that no one hears it, and then they stop clapping, and then there is no more clapping, though you can still hear it, or think you still hear it: the soft thud of finger pads in your head. It is strange, this communication and care between species. It occurs to you that animals only speak when it is necessary or beautiful, but you let that thought go, because it's not very interesting, and release your body into the heaviness of the wood, a heaviness so heavy that it almost lifts you up, a kind of buoyancy.

It's pointless to wonder whether you know anyone here or what anyone thinks or what they recognize as real. All is softness and heaviness, but within that heaviness, an easy lightness, which is peculiar to these bears and their way of life. And now the sun has set, and the world has turned its back on you, so that the inside grows bright and full but also more empty and spacious. The light isn't bright enough to illuminate anything outside of its domain, so you must wait for something to pass within the light to see it, and when it passes out again, it ceases to exist.

It's snowing now, and some of the snow is drifting under the door. One of the bears has obtained a push broom and is trying to sweep it back out, but he isn't very successful, and it keeps coming back in. He isn't concerned and laughs as he does this, and a few other bears laugh too, but in a good-spirited and cheerful way, because they know if they were in his position it would be the same way. The snow is indifferent and does as it must, and no bear could overcome it, and they know this and laugh. When one bear gets tired, another takes his place, and when that bear gets tired, another takes his place, and so on, until the snow stops or the wind stops blowing it under the door. The snow has now turned to ice and is tinkling against the glass and blowing open the shutters.

These bears are smaller than normal bears and have to stand on their toes to secure the shutters, or sometimes one will get down on all fours and another will stand on his back. They wear sleeping caps on their heads, and some of them have vests and wooden shoes. They don't actually sleep as much as you would think, because they work in such a relaxed and gentle way that it's not a big deal to be awake. The difference between sleeping and waking is not too great; in fact, they are hardly aware of any difference, and if you could get them to speak in your language, even then they would not understand. They sleep and at the same time are working with no goal or destination in mind and no desire for achievement or progress. And yet they are almost always moving slowly and deliberately, a laconic lumbering through space that seems inefficient but isn't actually. It feels good to move that way, and they don't care about beauty. And yet they are beautiful, in their own way, and always at the center of their own bodies, even if they are living on the margins of a world.

And they are kind, truly kind, and allow humans to sleep in their beds when they have nowhere else to go. They would never think of selling anything but give it all away and demand nothing in return but loyalty and love.

Domination is the one thing they will not tolerate. Though they seem like gentle creatures and open to all kinds of human faults and foibles, exploitation is not to their liking. If it is found to be taking place under their auspices, they move with the blinding force of justice and execute the offender on the spot. They never hesitate or make any exceptions for the sake of mercy, for there are certain people who must exert power over others, and it cannot be helped, and it cannot be cured, and it must be met with swift and final action, or it will spread, and all will be in chains while one or two go free.

Then the bears open the doors of the cathedral and throw the body out into the cold. They clear the blood from the floor and continue their work, and the humans fall asleep in the safety and softness of their beds, and the lights go out.

MARIE

I

THE NUNS SEPARATE THE CHILDREN INTO GROUPS: the filthy ones, the stupid ones, and the quiet ones. The filthy ones they check for lice. The stupid ones they interrogate. The quiet ones they keep as "helpers." The children stumble around the courtyard, like dazed animals. Their hair is tangled. Their clothes are torn. They haven't eaten for a couple of days. Some of them were packed into buses and driven across the state. Others flew on military planes, but those were just as crowded. It's early winter. The courtyard contains two trees and a swimming pool covered with a tarp. One end has come loose and is flapping in the wind. The trees are bare. It's beginning to snow. The nuns make an extraordinary show of discipline to conceal the fact that they are afraid. Afraid of the winter, afraid of the war, but mostly afraid of the children.

At last, a man arrives. His name is Mr. Scott. He's dressed in blue jeans and a heavy brown jacket. He has tools in his hands. The nuns thank the heavens for sending Mr. Scott. They form a circle around him and escort him over to a blue metal door set into one side of the courtyard. "See," one of them says, "there's no handle." She looks expectantly at Mr. Scott and slides her hand over the spot where the handle should be. Mr. Scott chuckles. He takes a crowbar and pops the door open. The nuns stand back. They marvel at this. The helpers walk over to inspect the scene, but the nuns say, "Stand back! Stand back!" Mr. Scott walks through the blue door with a flashlight and descends the stairs. They hear the clanking of pipes and the whir of gas through the walls. When Mr. Scott comes back up, they first see his shadow flickering on the wall. Then the man himself, smiling. "Furnace is back on," he says warmly. The nuns kiss him and say, "God bless you. God bless Mr. Scott." Before he leaves he asks them, "Is that all I can do for you gals?"

The hotel is humming now. The nuns move the children into their rooms, four to a room, girls on the first floor, boys on the second. "Why do the boys get the second floor?" one of the girls whines. "Because boys are bad," one of the nuns says, "and God needs them to be closer to heaven so he can keep a better eye on them." The girl does not accept this at first. "And the ice machine is on the first floor," the nun adds, handing the girl a bucket. The girl lifts the lid off the ice bucket and says, "O-kay." Mr. Scott brought supplies. The helpers unload clean sheets and carry them to the rooms. Then they return for the vacuum cleaners. The nuns test the water in the showers. "Is it hot?" one of them asks. "As hot as it's ever going to get," another answers.

They undress the children and throw them into the shower. The children scream, "It's cold! It's cold!" and hop from one foot to the other. The girls hug themselves. The boys cup their crotches with their hands to shield themselves from the cold water. "You'll get used to it," the nuns say. The helpers bring towels, bars of soap, and underwear. They made a mistake at the warehouse and only sent girls' underwear: pink panties with horses and flowers printed on them. The boys complain. "I won't wear it," one of them says, tossing his underwear off the balcony. "I'd rather go naked." The underwear lands in the branches of the tree. One of the nuns looks up through the branches and scolds him. "That's perfectly good underwear," she says.

It takes a long time to get the tangles out of their hair. Before it's all done, they've broken three combs and four children cried and one of them swore and received a spanking. But now the hotel's all warm and glowing, and the lights in the courtyard have come on, and the children have been fed and are watching television before they go to bed. They sit cross-legged on the floor, and the blue light from the television flashes across their faces. The nuns have convened in the courtyard to discuss the day's happenings. The snow isn't much, barely an inch, but there will be more. They sweep a path from the gate to the doors and then, out of zealotry, sweep the rest of the courtyard. Two of them hoist a wooden crucifix into the air and hold it against the trunk of the tree, while a third takes out a hammer (lifted from Mr. Scott's toolbox while the rest of the nuns were kissing him), and nails it into place. "There," she says, "perfect," and stands back to admire her work. "We need a priest," one of the nuns says, and the rest of them nod and say, "We surely do." Then they have their dinner in the courtyard at two tables pushed together and covered with a wool blanket. They eat cold chicken on paper plates with little packets of mustard, bags of Fritos, and cans of Pepsi from the vending machine. Bits of food get stuck in their yellow teeth. "We're going to need toothbrushes," one of them says, and another writes that down on a list. Once they're done eating, the nuns go to each room to put the children to bed and lock them in for the night. They keep the keys on a ring that hangs from the waist, hidden by their habits. Only one nun stays in the courtyard to clean up. She knocks the crumbs into a black trash bag but saves the plates. Then she ties the top of the bag in a knot and sets it next to the brooms. She forgets to lock the gate, and once everyone is in bed, a resourceful tabby pushes it open and looks both ways before sauntering over to the table to steal some fallen food.

When they wake up, they can see their breath. The furnace went out in the night. The nuns groan inwardly. Outwardly they make a stoic display of strength for the children. The children huddle together and let their teeth chatter. The nuns agree: they must send someone for help. One of the children. They can't go themselves. There's too much work to do, and besides they're old and would have trouble scrambling over the rubble and across blown-up bridges and around land mines. Better to send one of the kids instead. "It'll be an adventure!" one of the nuns says while the rest pray for guidance. At last, God tells them his bidding. She's one of the quiet ones. She is bright and obedient. Her body is lithe and athletic, capable of dodging bullets. She's thirteen years old. Her name is Marie.

"Shouldn't we send one of the boys?" one of the nuns asks, but that nun is duly chastised by the others for questioning God's commands.

They give Marie a day's worth of food in a rucksack, a heavy coat (not bulletproof but durable), boots that are a tad too big, a highway map, and a gun. "It's not a toy," one of the nuns says and shows Marie how to point it away from her while she's loading the barrel. "Make sure it locks into place," she says, and Marie listens attentively for the click. She's a good girl. She'll do fine. Some of the boys whine and say it's not fair. "I didn't ask for this," Marie says, arranging the supplies in her rucksack. "It's God's doing, not mine." The boys say God doesn't always know what's right, and Marie scolds them and tells them that's blasphemy. The nuns tell her where to go. It's a day's walk there and back. She can be back by nightfall if she hurries. "Tell them the furnace is out, and also we need toothbrushes." One of the boys whines, "It's not fair, it's not fair," until one of the nuns slaps the back of his head.

She's to follow the highway for two miles until she reaches the river. If the bridge is intact, she can cross it. If not, she'll have to walk a mile north to the Walmart where the riverbed dries out and find a shallow part to cross. On the other side, the highway picks up again, but it'll be faster if she takes Route 9 straight to headquarters. She won't be able to see it. It's underground. There's a password, and Sister Ida whispers it into her ear. She's not to utter it aloud to anyone but the mole in the hole. She's not to dillydally but to go straight there and back. And if she sees a soldier from the Red Army she should run, and if he comes close, she should shoot him. Sister Ida says, "See that tree there? That's the enemy," and Marie takes aim and shoots him right through the eye. "No," Sister Ida says, resting her hands on Marie's shoulders. "Lower. Through the heart."

II

She can see Walmart for a long time before she reaches the parking lot. It's not open anymore, but there may be things left on the shelves. The windows are boarded up, but the boards are broken in places. She crawls through an opening. It's dark inside. Her boots splash in water. The pipes must have broken. She can't see anything at first, but after a while her eyes adjust: there are rows and rows of empty shelves and bats hanging from the rafters, hundreds of them, with their wings wrapped tightly around their chests like blankets. Pink veins twitch in their wings. The grey down ripples. They open their eyes. Marie turns and runs to the sound of wings flapping. When she is halfway across the parking lot, she looks back and sees a dozen bats fly out of the hole, circle her head, decide she's not worth it, and return to their lair. Bats! My God. She thought she would find food or maybe a Barbie doll.

Marie decides to get serious. No more messing around. She follows the river until she can see rocks big enough to hop across. She jumps, steadies herself, almost falls, but catches a branch and finally swings herself to the other side. The sun is overhead. Must be noon. She follows Route 9 through cornfields, the corn unharvested and overgrown with weeds. She looks for the pyramid of rocks that Sister Ida said would be there. And indeed it is. She turns into the cornfield and walks sixteen paces. Here she finds the manhole. She presses her lips to the top of the manhole and whispers the password. The manhole opens. The mole asks: "Who speaks?" And Marie says: "A messenger. From the Highway Motel." She descends into headquarters.

From here the tedious details of bureaucracy take over. Marie stands in line. There are other children from other hotels on errands of their own. They compare stories. Kinds of soap. Bedtimes. That kind of thing. "They gave you a gun?" one girl says in alarm. Marie shrugs. She thinks about telling the girl about the bats but decides to keep that to herself. The line moves. They are out of the furnace repair form, so she handwrites a request:

> Dear U.S. Military People,
>   Our furnace is broken at the Highway Hotel. We are cold and getting colder. Mr. Scott came yesterday to fix it, but the pilot light went out in the night. Please send help we also need toothbrushes.
>   Love, Marie

Love doesn't seem like the right way to close the letter, but she can't think of what else to write so she leaves it. Then she hands it to the woman behind the counter, who reads it once and stamps it urgent.

Back above ground daylight is fading. It is snowing heavily. She must hurry. She dashes through the cornfields, skips across the river, and is back in no time, leaving footprints behind her in the snow-covered parking lot of Walmart. It's dark now, about six o'clock. The parking lot lights come on. That's strange. There's blood on the snow. And footprints. Leading to the bat's lair. It's none of your business, a voice says in her head, but she ignores that voice and follows the trail of blood to the entrance of Walmart. Just a peak, she says. And then straight back to the hotel. No harm done. There's a hole in the wood. The inside is brightly lit, just as it had been before the war, with large, domed fluorescent lights hanging from the ceiling. Someone has mopped up the water. The floor is clean and dry. Inside men are moving the shelves, turning them over, and then filling them up with hay. The bats are gone. The men are dressed in dark clothing, and the clothing looks hairy. There are tiny hairs growing out of the cloth, and it makes the clothes looks soft. Once they are done filling the shelves with hay, some them of lie down in it. Then two of the hairy men bring another man out in handcuffs. The blood came from him. He's shot and bleeding from the shoulder. They patched him up but didn't do a very good job, and now they're taunting him. They call him a pussy and a bitch, and one man sticks his tongue in the prisoner's ear. The prisoner wipes his ear, and at the same time, by instinct, Marie wipes hers, remembering Sister Ida's kiss earlier in the day. They tell the prisoner they'll keep him as a pet. He's a handsome man, with slender bones and fine features, though his face is marred with cuts. His hair is blonde and comes to his shoulders; the ends touch the tops of his collar bones. Marie has never seen anyone so beautiful...but hasn't she seen him before? She blushes. She's ashamed of seeing him humiliated like this and then angry but also afraid, because how can she help him? The hairy men lead him to a cage in the corner of the warehouse, close to the entrance, and shove him inside. They lock the cage with a heavy padlock and return to their beds of hay. Then someone shouts, "Lights out!" and the lights go out, one at a time, until it's completely dark.

Marie waits for a long time before deciding what to do. She takes off her boots and climbs in her socks over the wood and into the warehouse. Quieter that way. She follows the wall with her hand. If I hold onto this, they can't see me, she tells herself, and the trick works and calms her mind. In the corner she finds the cage. She falls to her knees and takes the gun out of her rucksack. Now her eyes have adjusted and she can see into the cage. He's lying on his side, looking away from her. She reaches through the bars and cups her hand around his mouth. The tip of his tongue touches the back of her palm. And with the other hand she slips the gun into his. He understands. He turns to look at her, and she throws a note at his feet. "I need the gun back," it says and instructions on where to meet.

III

The furnace is back on. The children say "Hurrah for Marie!" and hug her when she returns. Sister Ida says she's done well, but don't get a big head about it. "I won't," Marie promises, and another child holds a stick over her head. It's a head-shrinking stick. Marie pulls her hair back against the scalp to make her head smaller, and everyone laughs, even Sister Ida. Later, after dinner, Marie goes to see Sister Ida in her room. "I have something to confess." "What is it, my dear?" "I've lost the gun," Marie says, feigning guilt. Even her cheeks blush. She looks down at her feet. "I dropped it by accident into a ditch. By then it was dark. I crawled around for a long time, feeling around in the darkness, but I couldn't find it and gave up." Sister Ida frowns. "Did you feel anything?" she says. "Yes," Marie says.

"The ground felt like skin with little hairs sticking out, like the hair on a man's back." Sister Ida says, "Go on. Is that all?" "I could only feel the space around the gun but not the gun itself." Sister Ida says she must return first thing in the morning to retrieve it. Marie agrees. "I know it's still there," she says.

On the way to meet him, she tries to remember his face. She thinks of what he will say, how grateful he will be, and how he might reward her, how they will run away together to Canada or, better yet, to Mexico. When she arrives at the spot, he's not there. But then she hears his voice. "Over here." She told him to meet her under the trees by the dump, but he's hiding in one of the boxcars. It's the perfect hiding spot. Inside he's sitting on the floor. His eye are closed. He's holding his head in his hands. His face and shoulders are covered in sweat. "Here's your gun," he says, when he sees her. "Now go away." "But you'll die!" Marie says, coming to his side. She takes the gun—it feels lighter than before—and sets it on the floor. "I don't care," he says. "I want to die." Marie brings her hand to his forehead. She loves to touch him and would go on touching him, but he pushes her away. "You're burning up," she says. Her heart is beating faster. She knows where she's seen him before. But she doesn't tell him now. She kisses his face. He can't run away from her. He has to accept her kisses. "I'll be back," she says. "I'm going to save you."

IV

The war is hell. Another thousand dead in Chicago. New York is under water. Los Angeles is in flames. The news comes to them from the regiments passing through this part of the country, few and far between. When soldiers stay at the hotel, the children must sleep four to a bed and get kicked in the night by their bedmates. But it occupies the nuns and makes it easy to sneak away. And it's easy to steal supplies from the army trucks, which is what Marie does this morning on her way to the dump. She brings two blankets, aspirin, and a medical kit. She also steals food from the kitchen: hotdogs, chips, and a bag of apples. The day is warm and clear. The snow has melted. She knows he will be alive. She finds him in the same spot, still covered in sweat, and he's shivering, which is not good, but at least he is alive. His skin looks greyish blue. His hair is greasy. His eyes have receded into the sockets, and his skin is a thin cover for his bones. But even like this he is handsome, and each time Marie touches him it gives her an electric shock.

His temperature is 104—dangerously high. Marie spreads one blanket out on the floor of the boxcar and has him lie down on it. She cleans and dresses the shoulder wound. It appears to be healing. That's good. She soaks a clean handkerchief in alcohol and rubs his chest, arms, and forehead. Alcohol reduces fever. He looks better already. He murmurs something and rolls onto his side, bringing his knees into his chest. Marie takes out a comb and cleans the dirt out of his hair. "No," he says. "You're hurting." "I'm helping you," Marie says. "I'm a friend." She puts the aspirin in his mouth, and when he spits them out, she crushes them into a powder and puts it under his tongue. She washes his feet and covers him with the other blanket. His breathing grows deeper and more even. That's good, Marie thinks, clapping her hands. He will live. The clap rings out in the boxcar, but he goes on sleeping. The boxcar is surprisingly warm. The decomposing matter from the dump produces an incredible amount of heat. She won't have to worry about him freezing in the night. She cleans the floor and sets a candle burning. Next to this she lays out the food and water. She stands in the doorway for a minute, watching him sleep. A strange feeling is coming over her, something she has never felt before, something like possession.

The children annoy her. When she is alone she thinks only of him, counting down the minutes until she sees him again. The children wonder why she isn't playing anymore. Because she thinks she's too good. They can feel her disdain. She spends all her time in a corner of the courtyard, talking to two of the soldiers. Now that she has a man of her own, she feels like she understands them. She asks them about the war, and they say it will probably go on forever, because evil can't ever be rooted out completely and always comes back in a different form. "That's the nature of terrorism," one of the solider says. "Are they terrorists?" Marie asks. "Of course. Don't you know that? Don't they teach you anything around here?" "They're rats," the other soldier says. "Cowards and rats." "What do they want?" Marie asks. "They want chaos," the soldier says, holding his belt with both hands. Marie looks at the belt buckle. It's big and gold and engraved with the phrase, "Freedom for All." "I like your belt," Marie says. "Can I touch it?" The soldiers look at each other and laugh nervously. She's a nice girl but kind of strange.

All the time she is away, she is thinking about him, and when she sees him, his appearance doesn't disappoint but gives her more fodder for her fantasies. His eyelashes, for instance, combined with his nimble hands and a mole below his shoulder blade that she hadn't noticed before. Their relationship has gone in reverse: by the time he learns her name, she has already examined his body many times over and claimed every part of it for herself. When she finds him, she is ecstatic. He has woken up in the night and eaten the food. His face looks fuller. His fever has broken. He is alive, and it's all because of her. She lays out a fresh round of food and throws the remains into the dump. On the way back, she finds a mirror, a white pitcher, and a chair still intact. She hangs the mirror from a nail in the side of the boxcar. It looks nice. The sight of herself standing next to the sleeping man gives her a thrill. It suddenly occurs to her that she could do whatever she wanted to him, something cruel even, because he's completely helpless. But she would never do that. He is everything to her. She opens the door wide to let the air in. She sets the pitcher on the floor next to the food and fills it with juniper. She straightens out the blankets and sets the chair on the other side of him. She sits there for a long time watching his chest move up and down, studying the lines of his body under the blanket. His breathing is calm and deep.

When he wakes up, he groans and coughs, and spits out a greenish substance onto the floor. "Where are my clothes?" he says. "I took them to the hotel," Marie says. "They were dirty. Don't worry. I'll bring them back." He rolls over and looks at her. She is sitting in the chair looking down at him with big eyes, like a child looking at koi in a pond. "Who are you?" he asks. She is stunned. How could he not know her? It stings to be ignored by the object of your desire. There's nothing worse. "Don't you remember me?" she asks. "We've met already. My name is Marie." He examines her face but doesn't recognize it. No, he's never seen this girl before.

When she returns to the hotel, the soldiers are standing at attention in the courtyard. The nuns and children are all upstairs standing on the balcony with their hands resting on the railings. One of the soldiers is reading the news: the president has left the country with his wife and children. This isn't really news, though. Everyone's been talking about it for weeks. Still, the soldiers and nuns feign shock. All of the rich Americans left months ago; they sought asylum in Sweden and France. Some of them went to Brazil, and a few took up residence in Argentina. Others refused to disclose their location. They owned islands, so they didn't have to say where they were going. On the forms they wrote "vacation home." Now the only people left are the ones who can't leave and the ones who are crazy enough to stay. That's what the soldiers say. The real Americans, the ones who love this country. They don't answer to the president, anyway. The soldiers answer to the commander. The nuns answer to God. The children don't answer to anyone. Marie watches from the gate. She can't go in now; everyone would see her. The soldier reads the itinerary and a few other announcements about military procedures that don't make any sense to her. The last announcement gets her attention. There's a wanted man in the area, they say. He escaped from confinement a week ago. "He's a dangerous man," the soldier says, though it's clear he doesn't have firsthand information and is reading this off the report from headquarters. "We have reason to believe he's somewhere in the vicinity." Then he reads a physical description of the man, but Marie doesn't need to hear it. She already knows it's him.

After the announcements, they eat, and after they eat, the nuns put the children in their pajamas while the soldiers sit at the wooden tables in the hotel rooms drinking whiskey and playing cards. They are each allowed two drinks only. The nuns enforce this rule without exception. They hold the keys to the liquor cabinet, and the soldiers must go through the nuns if they want their whiskey. Tonight the televisions are working again. They're playing a movie about a prison break that goes badly. They sit on the bed in their pajamas, their mouths open wide. Marie gets bored and sits at the table with the soldiers. "What do you know about him?" she asks. "About the wanted man?" "He's a maniac," one of the soldiers says. "Totally depraved, beyond redemption." "What did he do?" Marie asks. "What's so bad about him?" The soldier leans in close, and holds his cards in front of his face so that the others can't hear him. "He killed innocent people, good people." Marie looks away. "Maybe they deserved it," she says. "Don't ever say that," the soldier says. "Curse your own mother if you like, but never, ever say that," he says. "I don't have a mother," Marie says. "That's silly," he says. He's exasperated with the girl and accidentally sets his cards down faceup, so everyone can see them. It's a bad hand, and now the other players know it. "Everyone has a mother." "Not me," she says. "I never did." "What about a father, then?" She thinks for a minute. "No," she says. "Not that either."

After the movie is over, Sister Ida has Marie collect the whiskey glasses and wash them in the kitchen. The children go to bed. The soldiers stay up a little later smoking and talking in the courtyard. Marie decides she must see him again tonight. She closes the back door to the kitchen but leaves it unlocked. When she reaches the dump, she can see the opening to the boxcar lit by candlelight. It's so bright, amplified by the mirror on the wall. He's awake. He's moving around. She says from the entrance, "Quick, put out the candle," and in an instant they are in darkness. "Did you bring my clothes?" he says. "Yes," she says and hands them to him. She can hear him dressing in the dark, and the sound excites her. "They know that you're here," she says. "Then I should leave," he says. "No! You can't!" she says, and finds his arm in the darkness and holds it tight. "I love you. I can't live without you." He pats her head in a brotherly way. He laughs. "That's silly," he says. "You don't even know me." "Yes, I do," she says. "I saw what those men were doing to you, and I gave you my gun." "And I took care of you even when you said you wanted to die." She is crying now. "And I saw you in a movie," she says. "I know who you are. Your name is Ronny Coco. You were in that movie about surfers. I watched it so many times. And I cried when you died in the end. I knew you would come back. I knew I would meet you some day." He is moved but also disturbed by this. "What happens in the movie?" "There's a wave coming," she says. "A big one. It only happens once every hundred years. It's legendary. No one has ever survived it before, though many people have tried. You tell the other surfers they're dumb for even trying. You're a fatalist—in the movie. But then something happens: the wave comes early, a few weeks early, when no one's expecting it. And so you have to surf the wave anyway, even though you tried to avoid it." "And I die in the wave?" "No, you survive. That's the amazing part. You're the first to survive it. But now you've seen things, like the inside of the universe, and everyone in the seaside town is afraid of you, even the girl you're dating and her parents, and in the end the people kill you, because they don't want to know the truth." He is a little bit afraid of her. At the same time, he's fond of her and grateful for saving his life. And he's charmed by her story, as crazy as it is. He sits down on the floor, and she sits next to him, and rests her head on his shoulder. "I'm not Ronny Coco," he says. "I'm a soldier in the Red Army. My name is—well, I can't tell you my name. If you knew it you'd be liable to tell someone." "No, I'd never," she says. "Even under torture?" he says. "Even if they poured boiling hot water on your head? Or put your hand in the fire?" "Not even then!" she yells. "Not even if they made me stand outside in a snowstorm! Or tied my arms and legs to horses and sent them running to the four corners of the Earth!" He says he will tell her then. "No," she says, "Don't. I don't need to know. I already know everything about you." She sits in his lap and kisses him, and he lets her kiss him, because how could he say no.

V

His name is Benjamin Rock. The soldiers tell her the next morning. They are distributing flyers with his face on it, and they say his name again and again, like an incantation. They have German Shepherds on leashes, and they give the dogs a bit of his clothing to smell. The dogs go straight to Marie's legs, sniff her, and bark furiously. They stick their snouts up her skirt, and tickle her with their wet noses. The soldiers think it is a mistake and call the dogs off. "Sorry, Marie," they say. "I guess their sniffers are broken." The name doesn't sound right to her: Benjamin Rock. He doesn't look like a Benjamin Rock. He looks like a Ronny Coco. She wonders if he's even the right person. His photograph is blurry. It might not be him. But the soldiers are eager to find him. They say when they find him the war will end. Or soon after that, they say, because he'll surely be executed. "What did he do?" Marie asks, trying to hide her fear. "That's not for you to know," they say. They are rabid, the soldiers, the nuns, even the children are ready for the kill.

She goes to see him once more. "They're coming," she says. "Do you still have the gun?" he says, and she says, "Yes." "Then give it to me." "No. First tell me what you did. Why are they after you? Why did those hairy men capture you and put you in a cage in Walmart?" "You saw. They wanted to humiliate me, that's all." "But why?" "Because this is a war, and I'm on the other side." "But that can't be all. You have something inside of you. They want it." She touches his sides and his back, looking for something, she doesn't know what. "That's a fantasy," he says. "You've got to grow up." He reaches for the gun, but she snatches it away. "I know who you are," she says. "I know more than you know." Now she's pointing the gun at him. "Get in the corner," she says. "Now!" He walks to the corner of the boxcar and crouches down with his hands above his head. "Before you go, say that you love me." He hears the sounds of dogs barking. He shakes his head. Of course, the whole thing has been a setup. Now he's a terrorist and also a pervert. They'll hang him by Sunday and probably sooner.

A Whole New Man

EVERYONE WAS WAITING FOR SOMETHING TO HAPPEN. The people in the stands stood very still, as if any sudden movement might determine the outcome of the game, while the officials gathered around the hole in the field, which had only moments ago opened up and swallowed the quarterback, Booney Starr.

The replay video showed Booney in the final seconds of the game retreat from the pocket, three, maybe four feet, to the forty-yard line, bring the ball back, and make an incredible throw, maybe the best of his career, to his receiver who, with three defenders on him, somehow managed to catch the ball and somersault into the end zone.

The throw was good, but the quarterback was gone.

He fell through the Earth and landed in his bed as a woman named Britney watching internet porn.

What the fuck, he thought as he dressed, jumped into his car, and raced back to the stadium to see whether his team had won the game. They had in fact won the game, due to his extraordinary athleticism and crunch-time leadership, and were accepting the trophy on his behalf. A few groundskeepers were already filling in the hole in the field.

"Booney would have wanted us to celebrate," said the coach with tears in his eyes.

Now Booney had almost forgotten his transformation and went to join his teammates on the stage but was tackled by several security guards and thrown out of the stadium. Well, what could he do? He got a job selling hotdogs at the stadium and dressed as seductively as possible, only to attract the attention of the general manager who, the following season, invited Booney to watch the season opener from his box seats high in the stands. Together they drank champagne and had a pretty good time, actually. After the game, the GM put his hand on Booney's thigh, kissed him, and invited him to his lake house for the weekend.

Well, how bad could it be? Booney wasn't a fag, but he wasn't completely against the idea, either. And he was a woman now, after all. Booney and the GM had the most incredible sex imaginable. Soon enough they were married and had three children together. Booney would advise the GM on the strategy and general direction of the franchise and because of his insider knowledge was able to maneuver the team into another three Super Bowl wins. The GM called Booney his good luck charm and showered him with gold and expensive clothing. All of the players wanted to sleep with Booney, and some of them did when the GM was on the road. Booney felt sort of bad about that, especially since he was pregnant again and did not know who the father was.

When the baby was born and was clearly not the GM's, he kicked Booney to the curb, keeping everything, including their children, in a vicious legal battle that was all over the tabloids. Booney wandered the streets with his black baby, each day looking for food and shelter and trying to scrape together a life. It was winter in Boston, and everyone was an asshole.

This probably would have been the death of him had he not one night leapt into the river with his little baby in a backpack.

The second before he hit the water, he was transformed back into his former self, and his baby was transformed into a football that he was cradling in the end zone.

He gently kissed the pigskin before tossing it to the fans, who were totally losing their shit.

FINNEY'S TALE

A CORPSE NAMED FINNEY RETURNED TO THE LIVING. He wasn't sure why. There must have been something he had forgotten to do. He brushed the dirt off his shoulders. He was wearing a nice suit, nicer than any he had owned when he was alive. The family must have pitched in to buy him one so that he would look presentable at his funeral. That was thoughtful of them.

It was easy to get out of his coffin because it was made of thin plywood. He just punched a hole in it and crawled out of the earth. They must have spent so much money on the suit that there was nothing left over for the coffin. He approved of those choices. Better to look good in your coffin, even a cheap coffin made out of plywood, than to have one of mahogany and look like a chump in it.

He felt fine. It was fall, and fall was his favorite season. He liked the little yellow locust leaves hanging on in the wind, not knowing what would happen to them, or where they would go. He walked through the gates of the graveyard and into the town. It was the same town, but many things were different. There was a car wash now. Its storefront looked like a giant shimmering tsunami wave about to crash into the street. Below that a few men and women were sudsing up their cars while their children sat inside and pointed at things. That was new, and there were banana posters hanging from the lampposts, advertising a new kind of banana. Those were new, too. The cars also looked new. They had soft, air-filled bladders to protect them from the dings and scratches that come with commuting in the modern world, or at least that's what the signs said that were attached to the backs of the cars.

But the cars went through streets instead of flying through the air and were still driven by humans, or the rough equivalent. Their clothes were not outrageous—they were the same as Finney remembered—but they shimmered, and shirts fell below the knee on both men and women. Their faces looked exactly as faces should look, only tweaked to make room for the future and obliterate the past. He thought he must have been dead for five years at the least, twenty at the most.

Finney walked through the town and said hello to the residents. No one seemed to mind or even notice that he was dead, or had been dead and brought back to life, if only temporarily.

He walked to his family's house and knocked on the door. A little girl answered and then called to her mother, who came to the door and told him that she and her family had lived there for many years, she had lost count, and did not know who had lived there before or when they left.

It's likely Finney's death had been a financial burden to his family, and the house had been repossessed by the bank. He felt so bad and wanted to make it up to them somehow.

He thought of his mother, first of all, who worked as a dishwasher all her life and did so without complaint, though sometimes she would steal plates from the restaurant, if only to bring them home and smash them against the wall. But that was only sometimes. Usually she exuded a deep and unspoken love for all living things, whether animal or vegetal. She surrounded herself with and fed off of them and kept them so close to her that they actually became inseparable from her, or indistinguishable, from an outside perspective. If she held a chick in her hand, as she often did, because she loved soft things, the chick would merge with her hand, and when she let it go, it would die. When she walked through a field, all of the grasses and wildflowers would annex themselves to her legs. All words were her words, whether they came out of her mouth or stayed inside her skull. She had a gift for this, filling everything that came near her with the delirium of her own mind, a delirium which did not originate in her head but was conferred upon her by a higher power, and she merely conveyed it, in her own way, a passive receptacle for a force that exceeded her, like a branch shaking in the wind.

Finney thought about his mother and tried to describe all this to the woman at the door, but she said she had to go because her daughter was getting into the cookies.

He knew it was a lie, but it didn't matter. The point had been made. Finney grew nostalgic for a life he could not remember and everything his mother and father had done for him. For instance, this nice suit, in which he had done nothing but decompose, and the funeral, where his sister probably spent her last dollar on a dozen white lilies. Though he hoped not, because he knew his mother hated lilies. They reminded her of funerals, and that would have been depressing to her. He hoped they bought carnations for him, an unusual choice for sure, but more cheerful and less expensive or even just a few peonies stolen from someone's garden or a bunch of leaves stuffed into a plastic bucket or whatever.

It didn't matter. What was important now was he was alive and could do it all over again, and better. But first he would have to get a job. He went to the car wash first; that would be nice, working outdoors and seeing all the happy people cleaning their cars. But the car wash was entirely automated, apart from the senior technician who directed the whole operation from his control booth at the top of the tsunami. He had a little microphone and spoke slowly into it, like a god of the mentally incapacitated, but could not convey Finney into the safety of employment. The senior technician wished him well. They would keep his application on file.

Then Finney went to the bank and asked there and the grocery store and a few other undesirable places. Finally, he went to the restaurant where his mother had worked for so many years as a dishwasher.

The restaurant had changed. It used to be a Mexican restaurant named Diablo's, and now it was a pizza place called Joe's. They changed the name and the food, but the walls were still covered with painted sombreros, and the manager was still the same.

When Finney mentioned his mother's name, the manager said, "Oh! Your mother! Your mother was a saint, the nicest lady in the world, and a hard worker, too." He handed Finney an apron and told him to start right away.

Finney liked washing dishes. He liked the warm water on his hands, and he liked looking at the bubbles. The plates came in covered with salad dressing and pizza sauce and went out shiny and new. It was comforting to know that he was doing the same thing his mother had done for so long, and he was standing in the same place his mother had stood. He thought he could even see the impression of her feet on the mat, and his feet were the same size as her feet. These dishes were like her children, and these forks her defense against the world, and Finney took great care with them and kept them free of all smudges.

He bore the dishes aloft, like a host, or an infant heir to her kingdom, and submerged each in the water and gave it his blessing. He felt a swell of pride for carrying on, in his own life, his mother's life's work, interrupted only by his death, which now seemed irrelevant. There was something so right about it, he would even go so far as to call it timeless that he should come back from the dead to do his mother's work and to do it so well. There would always be a demand for pizza, and as long as people ate pizza in restaurants, there would be dishes and therefore a dishwasher and a steady job for Finney and enough money to keep him alive, or at least not dead.

The cooks were mean and vindictive, but the waitresses were pretty and nice. They carried pizzas high on their shoulders and kicked in the swinging door when they left the kitchen but without upsetting the waitress coming in from the other side. This was a miracle to Finney, the physical dexterity of the living, how they moved with thoughtless grace toward anything they wanted, or whatever had been denied to them, which only increased their desire for it.

He began to try it too, to juggle a few coffee cups in the air—three, four, five at a time—and it came easily to him, because there was nothing to fear now. He would throw a plate across the room and be there to catch it, and he could balance seven forks in his open palm.

It was nice to be alive and it was nice to go home at the end of the day with a pocket full of money and a waitress on your arm.

The waitresses had incredible stamina, probably from being on their feet all day. Their shoulders were big and broad. All those years carrying heavy trays had made them strong.

One night after work Finney went home with one of the waitresses. Her name was Dot. They were watching a movie in her living room. The movie involved a pair of flight attendants who believed the pilot to be their father and were willing to hijack the plane to prove it. They weren't terrorists, just a couple of American girls who were angry and confused. It turned out, in the end, that the pilot wasn't a father to either of them, but they only found that out after the plane crashed and everyone died but them. The last shot of the movie showed the two flight attendants standing in the rubble with their blue uniforms torn open and little silk scarves around their necks, the sun setting behind them.

Dot thought the movie was predictable, but Finney found it moving and had to turn away to keep Dot from seeing him cry. But she saw anyway and said, "It's ok to cry, and I'm fine with it, but you should save your tears for something actually sad and not some dumb movie."

Finney didn't know what to say to that. He thought Dot was being insensitive. She looked away, and he watched her face rotate away from him and then return, like a gate swinging open and shut, signifying nothing.

Finney remembered his father then, partly from the movie and partly from Dot's expressionless face. His father had a face, a face like any other, but hidden from view. He always set himself at certain angles, so that Finney could hear his words but could not see his lips moving or his eyes turning in their sockets. He could only see the side of his father with his arm terminating in a gesture of some sort, rendered so perfectly that the words became irrelevant. There was a phone in the basement, a burgundy phone, and Finney's father spoke into the receiver. He remembered him eating a waffle once. And he put a little bit of it on a fork and stuck it in Finney's mouth.

"I knew your father," Dot said.

Finney ignored her and returned to his thoughts.

"Yeah, he used to come into the restaurant when it was Diablo's, and we would talk out back while your mom did the dishes."

Finney hoped she would stop, but she kept talking.

"He was my favorite customer, and I was his favorite waitress, and I was so alluring to him that he turned away from your mother and toward me. I gave him everything he wanted and he gave me everything I wanted. It was easy for both of us because we lived in basically the same world and saw the same things. The sun rose and set. Cars carried you to wherever you wanted to go, even against your will sometimes, but always with the assurance that you would end up somewhere. It may not be the place you intended, but it would be somewhere. Anyone could see that, in the day, a few cars and shopping carts, and at night those same shopping carts gathered under a streetlight, not the kind lining the street but in the parking lot to light the way wherever you were going. We were walking through one of those parking lots once. Your dad's car broke down, or ran out of gas, I can't remember, and we were walking through the lot, and those lights shone down on us. The shopping carts were under the light, three or four upright and one on its side. The lights flickered and went out then, and we couldn't see anything. I gave a long push into the darkness. He felt something moving, but the moment the lights came back on, nothing had changed because nothing wanted to change, under the circumstances. I think you died around that time, but I can't remember the details. I stayed at the restaurant, but he stopped coming, and then your mom moved away."

Finney wasn't listening. He was thinking about his work at the restaurant and how it had become dull. He looked at the bubbles but could not see himself in them. The water blackened and became wet, wetter than it already was. He plucked a blonde hair from the surface of the water. He didn't want it to end up in someone's food. He watched Dot's hand run along the wood paneling. She took off her pants and then her underwear and stood over Finney with her big body. He put his hand between her legs, and her hair fell forward against his face, tumbling blonde. The barrettes fell out of her hair, but Finney reached out and caught them before they hit the ground. He might stay at his job but not for longer than a month. Then Dot came, or pretended to come, and Finney finished on her back.

The rest came easily. His body was falling apart. He had to quit his job because he was afraid his hands would dissolve in the water.

Then Dot said, "You know, I'm pretty sure your mom moved to Detroit, and you've earned enough money to buy a bus ticket, and that's the bus—it's leaving right now."

Finney got on the bus, paid his fare, and waved at Dot from the window. The bus drove all night. Finney couldn't see anything except parking lots with lights and shopping carts underneath, conspiring with each other, waiting for the lights to go out.

In Detroit, everyone was gone except his mother, who lived in a house between two tall buildings. She spent her time gardening and didn't mind Finney's presence, though she didn't recognize him as her son. She was kind to him, but it was the kindness of a stranger. He talked to her about Dot and his father and that night in the parking lot, and she listened but did not respond, as if he were relaying the plot of a not very interesting film.

They lived for a while like that, and Finney came to know her not as his mother but as his child. She had come out of his body and would die many years after he had already passed away, feeling like an orphan in her last years, like she had no one to turn to, and Finney felt sorry for leaving her, although he was dead and unable to feel anything.

And when he finally found her in the garden, facedown in the dirt, it was easy to bury her. He didn't even bother to get a shovel but scooped a little bit of dirt on her back with one of his shoes. Then she stirred for a second—not quite dead—and rose to her knees, and Finney was so startled that he had to hold onto a nearby tree branch to steady himself, but the weight was too much; the branch snapped and swung forward in his hand and knocked his mother out for good. He had to bury her again, but the second time was easier than the first.

THE BLACK BEAST

My cousin Amanda was working as a secretary for a company that produced, marketed, and sold customized medals and trophies, mostly for youth soccer leagues and adult bowling teams but also, on occasion, for the military and marathon races. Amanda's office was on the top floor of the tallest building in town, which wasn't very tall, actually, since the town was small and the downtown, where the company was located, consisted of only a few buildings.

One day, Amanda was looking out the window and onto the courtyard where a couple of employees were having their lunch. As soon as they departed, Amanda noticed another figure, bigger than a dog but smaller than a bear, burying something behind the gazebo. As soon as it had finished covering the hole, the animal ran away.

"What the hell was that?" said Steve, Amanda's boss, who had been watching the whole thing from the doorway.

"Some kind of black beast," Amanda said.

Steve laid his hand on Amanda's shoulder and told her to find out what the black beast had buried.

During her lunch break, Amanda went out to the court-yard with a small shovel and started digging. She looked up and could see Steve watching from the window. A light rain was falling. Inside the hole was the body of a rodent. Amanda took the body, carried it up four flights of stairs, and threw it onto Steve's desk.

Steve examined the carcass with great care before handing Amanda a trophy.

The next day, the black beast returned to its hole, only to find the trophy of a dead rodent instead of its dinner.

Steve tells this story to potential clients and at company dinners to great fanfare and applause.

THE OTHER SIDE
OF THE CHICKEN DOOR

I ONCE KNEW A MAN named Derrick who worked five days a week in a chicken processing plant and, on the sixth and seventh days, drove a taxicab around town. That's how we met, actually. I was his passenger, and he was my driver, and I used to call Derrick to get me to places I couldn't get to by bus or by foot.

Once Derrick told me what he did at his other job. He stood all day next to a wide, black conveyor belt. The chickens, who were headless, would come down the belt, a hundred or more at a time, and Derrick would have to grab them by their feet and hang them on metal hooks, which were moving along on a chain above Derrick's head. The chain whisked the hooked and headless chickens away, around a bend, and through a little door, where they disappeared from view. Then a hundred more chickens would tumble down the conveyor belt, and the whole process would start over again.

Derrick didn't know what happened on the other side of that door.

"Someone else's problem," he said.

Then one day Derrick was at work, moving as quickly as he could to hang those chickens, when the chain jammed, and the chickens stopped moving. No one else was around so Derrick had to crawl on top of the conveyor belt and through the little door to see what the problem was. He felt around in the darkness, although he wasn't sure what he was feeling for, when his hand landed on another person's hand, which was resting on the conveyor belt.

"Oh, sorry," Derrick said.

"I thought I was the only one here," the voice said.

"No, I work here, too."

"On the other side?"

"Yeah."

"How much do you make?"

"Eight and a quarter. You?"

"Eight and a half."

At that moment, the chain started moving again, along with the conveyor belt, which moved Derrick and the other man through the tunnel and dumped them out on the other side.

The other side of the chicken door looked completely different. The walls were blue instead of green, and the equipment was new and shiny.

"This side's better," Derrick said. The other man just shrugged and went back to his work, which consisted of taking the headless chickens and dropping each one into an acid bath, the purpose of which was to remove the feathers. He had to wear big pink rubber gloves and protective footwear in order to keep himself safe.

Derrick went over to him. He looked like every other person in the world, only happy.

Soon after that encounter, Derrick put in a request to work on the other side of the chicken door, but his request was repeatedly denied by the management. Now he drives his taxicab seven days a week and is barely getting by.

I tell you this story in the hope that you will patronize Derrick for your transportation needs. You can reach him by email or phone, or just stand on any street corner, and he will see you.

BISQUIT

THE RACETRACK BELONGED TO ANOTHER WORLD, although it was only a dozen miles away, sheltered from view of the city by a few low-lying hills—not quite mountains, but tall enough to give a protected feel to the racetrack and its grounds. Packed in the summer, empty in the winter, at the moment it looked like a snow globe scene, lonesome and enchanted, with a little man standing in the center of the gravel lot, waving at the truck as it rounded the bend and entered the gates of the racetrack park.

Nobody lived there except Mr. Buddy—everyone just called him Buddy—in a modest house behind the racetrack. Bisquit would now live there also, in a small though by no means squalid shed that Buddy had prepared just for this purpose. It was too soon to mix him with the other horses, Buddy explained as he led Bisquit from the truck and into the shed, but they were all excited to meet the new racehorse and see how he fared at the track.

Bisquit was glad to hear it. He felt calm and happy but also exhausted, and Buddy picked up on this immediately, wondering for a second whether he had been deceived by the banker's son. He had described Bisquit (granted, this was over drinks) as robust a horse as anyone could hope for, though with a slightly short stature that would prevent him, most likely, from ever being a truly great racehorse. Nevertheless, the banker's son said, he possessed the physical requirements and the intangibles, such as perseverance and high spirits, the will to win, mental toughness, etc., to be a very good racehorse, outrunning his potential and, at the very least, entertaining the crowds of racegoers who always rooted for the underdog and were willing to empty their pockets to see a loser win once in a while.

Buddy had been taken in by the rhetoric of the banker's son. At worst it would be a favor to his old friend, who appeared to be falling into financial ruin and could use a break, even if it came at Buddy's expense. But now as Buddy led this tired horse into his new home by a length of rope that sagged from the slowness of the horse, and the horse's head bent low like one defeated, he questioned the intelligence of his purchase: whether this horse would win anything for him or— God forbid—bring his misfortunes to Buddy's racetrack.

Still, the racetrack had done well that year. With the drought and starvation wages in the city, all of the farmhands and servants flocked to the racetrack, willing to toss away their last nickel at the chance to yell at some horses for a little while, and even though Buddy saw only a tiny fraction of that money, because almost all of it went to the investors who lived in another country and would never even consider going to a horse race (though they did from time to time watch the races on television, to remind themselves of what they were not), still, Buddy reasoned, the racetrack had done well that year, and he was so blessed to receive even a portion of that money that he really didn't care whether the purchase of Bisquit paid dividends or nothing at all. It was likely he would die within the week. Besides, Buddy had gotten into this business not for the money but because he loved horses, and here was a horse; that was undeniable. He seemed kind of sad, but there was strength in that sadness, and so Buddy found himself rooting for Bisquit—not in the crass races of this world, the ones that may bring money and fame but no real peace, but in the long spiritual slog that we all must join, whether we like it or not, the one that begins at birth and goes to the end of our days.

Buddy was given to this kind of thinking. He was a kind and Godly man and he truly loved horses. He called for a bucket of cold water and a pail of fresh oats, and he himself pulled a handful of clover out of the earth, mixing it in with the oats so that Bisquit would have some variety in his meal. He fluffed up the hay in Bisquit's shed so that he would have both a good meal and a restful sleep. Then he said good night and walked back to his house just as the sky was beginning to clear and the stars were coming out.

The next day Bisquit awoke completely refreshed, almost a new horse. By the time Buddy came to fetch him, he was already moving around in the shed, excited for what the day would bring. Buddy opened the doors, pulled hard at the reins, and Bisquit went willingly into his new life as a racehorse. All was behind him now: the farmer and his wife, the banker and his son—even the children were tokens of another life. It was spring and every living thing shot out of the earth; the aspens around the stadium, formerly bent under the weight of winter snow, grew in the night and stood eye to eye with the top of the stadium, small silver buds shooting out from their branches. All around was a bluish greenness that would have made Bisquit seasick had he mistaken it for water and not earth, and every kind of colored crocus and daffodil grew in the sun. Bisquit stood tall. His whole body shook and trembled in the early morning light. Buddy drove Bisquit up and down the fields, where his swift hooves cut a path through any kind of sharp grass or thistle, and as he ran the white snowbells shook their heads in appreciation. And when he whipped around the oak tree on the far end of the field or cleared a hurdle or two, he felt perfectly at ease in his new world and connected to a power he did not know he had.

It's true that Bisquit's short stature and wide head, along with his knock knees and hooves that were prone to stick in the mud, no matter how much you greased them, would prevent him from ever being a truly great racehorse, or even a good or decent one, or winning even a single race. Still he had a certain magnetic energy, an untapped potential, though what that might be exactly neither he nor Buddy really knew.

For the time being, it was such a joy for Buddy to watch Bisquit blossom into a good though never great racehorse that he didn't even bother to ask himself those questions. He threw himself into horse training with characteristic alacrity and passion but to an even greater degree, because Bisquit, though at times an incredibly slow learner and at other times slothful and vain, had that certain something, the intangible element, that transforms an impossibly defunct horse into an actually sort of decent horse that people want to see win, knowing full well he never will. Buddy could see that Bisquit had that element, the "it" factor, as he called it, and because of it, Buddy gladly spent every waking hour preparing Bisquit for the rigors of the racetrack, initiating him into his arcane though timeless repertoire of techniques that, if practiced diligently and executed properly, could raise any horse to the next level.

Bisquit took this all very seriously not because he had any interest in winning a horserace but because he felt a lingering obligation to his master. He heard Buddy talking on the phone one night—to whom he didn't know—and deduced from the conversation that the master's estate had been seized by the very bank that his father had founded, and he was unable in the end to even compensate Buddy for the cost of transporting Bisquit to the racetrack. And as he stood frozen in his shed, afraid to move lest the sound of moving hay obscure Buddy's words, the volatile mixture of love, fear, and humiliation conferred upon Bisquit by his master returned to him and renewed his desire to make the master proud. He wanted to bring honor to his name and his estate, even if the two-hundred-year-old house was at this very moment being razed to make room for an auto dealership, as he heard Buddy say with a chuckle. Bisquit looked to the sky and could see, just beyond the mountains, a little puff of dirty smoke and dust kicked up from the demolition. This saddened Bisquit, even as Buddy broke out into uproarious laughter, laughter that echoed all through the valley and sent every kind of spring songbird into the air. Bisquit resolved to make the master proud by being the best racehorse he could be; even if that was only a mediocre racehorse at best, he would follow the master's wishes through to the end.

Bisquit occupied himself with these thoughts for much of the night. At daybreak, he shot out of the shed and ran at a sprint across the field, or what felt like a sprint; any neutral person could see that he was moving at barely a trot. He rounded the oak tree, filling out nicely with tender leaves and casting dappled shade onto Bisquit's back. It felt so nice, and he grew tired, and sat down in the shade to rest for a moment.

Buddy watched all this from a nearby hill with so much admiration and love that he could barely contain himself. His training methods were unconventional in that he almost never came near Bisquit but shouted his commands from a little wooden stand that looked like a lifeguard stand. A big red-and-white striped megaphone hung from his waist if it was not in his hands. This way he could be sure that his own emotion would not be a distraction to Bisquit or impede in any way his natural growth. But all the same, Buddy couldn't restrain himself from clapping once or twice when Bisquit cleared another hurdle or punching the air when Bisquit rounded the oak tree, but slowly, and with so much modesty and physical restraint that Bisquit didn't notice. He could hear the claps but thought they were twigs falling from a tree far in the distance, of little concern to him.

Still, Bisquit knew Buddy loved him, and this love was so different than the crazed love of the farmer's wife or the distant, lavish, and ultimately brutalizing love of the banker's son. Buddy loved because he could love, because he truly loved horses, and Bisquit was a horse. But he was a special kind of horse,, though where that specialness resided and how it manifested itself, neither Buddy nor Bisquit could say exactly. Buddy had trained thousands of horses over the years, and almost all of them had been faster, smarter, better-looking, and even more industrious and spirited that Bisquit, but none had that special quality, a quality not to be identified by any objective measure or physical display, a quality that could not be expressed by even the most gifted of poets, a quality that surpassed language itself but that Bisquit nevertheless possessed.

The training was going well. The first race of the season was only a few weeks away, the spring was nearing its end, and soon enough the entire valley would be alive with revelers, everybody drunk, even the smallest child sipping a summer ale, and making their way to the racetrack. By this time, Buddy had become so wrapped up in training his new horse—even sleeping next to the shed at night in a tent so that he wasted no time in the morning, the time it took to walk from his house to the shed—that he had completely neglected his other duties as manager of the racetrack. The other horses had been locked up in their stables for weeks without food or water, the stadium was filled with trash, and the track itself was a bog: wet, soggy, and filled with sticky mud from all the spring rains. He had a lot of work to do and so little time to do it.

"Listen, Bisquit," he said, shaking him awake, for it was the middle of the night when this dawned on Buddy.

"I have a lot of work to do at the stadium. I've devoted all of my time to you this spring, and although I found that work enjoyable and rewarding in a way that I could never really articulate to anyone, even myself, still, I can't let my emotions rule the thing, otherwise there will be no race at all, and the world will never see what a fine racehorse you've become. You're on your own from now on, and I trust you'll keep up the regimen, though I can't imagine what would improve your performance at this point."

Bisquit couldn't hear him. He had grown fat and lazy. He needed at least twelve hours of sleep a day and would not have been able to wake up at night even if someone shot a rifle over his ear. He was confident in his abilities even as they atrophied more and more and, having no point of comparison, because he trained alone, became content easily and would hear no criticism from anyone. Around noon he wandered out into the open field. It was hot and the sky an unbelievably hot blue, almost a neon blue, cooled here and there by a few dollops of cloud. The hotness of the day created a haze in the valley, which almost obscured in the distance a small figure moving furiously around the racetrack like an ant in its hill. Bisquit watched as Buddy hauled enormous bags of garbage out of the stadium and tossed them into the dumpster. It didn't occur to him to help Buddy out, though he would never have turned his nose up at that kind of work when he was a lowly farmer's horse, or even a horse on an estate, but now he was a racehorse, and that kind of work was beneath him. And besides, he had to conserve his energy for the race. He took a few dainty trots around the oak tree, now fully leafed out, its shadow extending from one end of the field to the other, and called it a day, enjoying a few moments of summer repose.

For the next few weeks, Bisquit prepared in his way for the race, while Buddy ran around like a madman, tended the other horses, cleared all of the garbage out of the stadium and worked the track with his bare hands and a bag of sand, turning that sinkhole into solid ground. He was attaching the bright yellow flags, the annual racing flags, to the poles high above the stadium with a little bit of string that he hoped would hold on this fantastically windy day, when the first of the racegoers began filing into the stadium.

Buddy's work was complete. The stadium was immaculate. Even the most critical of racegoers could see that this was as clean as it had ever been. The concessions were stocked with every kind of edible: popcorn and pastries, roast beef and imported chesses, apples for the kids, and just that morning the town brewer had arrived, backing an impossibly large tankard of beer up to the stadium, where Buddy and the brewer were at the moment struggling to attach a long and unwieldy red hose to a nozzle in the stadium taproom.

The racehorses, despite months of neglect, had, under Buddy's guidance, returned to their former state and even improved upon it in a matter of weeks. They were milling about in the stables, waiting for the race to begin.

Soon enough the stadium was full to capacity, and Buddy had to turn hundreds of people away, directing them to a nearby tavern where they could watch the race on television. The people screamed and cursed but Buddy held his ground, reminding them that, although they would not be able to tell their children and grandchildren that they had been there on that historic day—the first race of the season! And one featuring a new horse named Bisquit!—still they would save themselves the price of admission and could apply those savings to more drinks at the tavern, where the drinks were half as expensive anyway, and the television was so large and clear that they could actually see more of the race than if they had seats in the front row.

The people were subdued by these words. Soon they dispersed, grumbling to each other, and Buddy went down to the stables to examine his horses. There were twelve in all: Roxie, Diamond, Johnny and Tommy, Helterskelter, Raymond, Princess, Big Dog, Little Dog, Trixie and Buck. All of the horses looked great, in peak physical condition, and were standing in a circle speaking in inscrutable horselike ways, chanting and whooping it up, to raise their courage and focus their energies for the race.

Buddy looked at his horses. He was so tired, he could barely stand or keep his eyes open and held onto the railing to keep himself from falling forward into a pile of hay or horse manure. He felt so happy but so very, very tired that he almost didn't notice when his twelfth horse, his most beloved horse, the horse for whom he had risked an entire racing season and public ridicule and disdain, nudged him in the arm. Bisquit entered the stable and joined the other horses, dressed in his blue racing attire.

The other eleven horses turned to look at him. Originally Buddy had planned to mix Bisquit with the other horses prior to race day, gradually and with great care, so as to avoid inciting petty jealousies and feuds, but that had all been forgotten either because he was so absorbed in training the new horse or because—and this was more likely—he wanted the new horse all to himself, unwilling to share him even with other horses, who, he feared, would love and covet Bisquit as much as he did.

Bisquit looked incredible. His daily training regimen, practiced sporadically and with little intensity and purpose, had over time produced an impressive equine specimen, and Buddy found himself falling in love with Bisquit all over again, reaching out like a sleepwalker to touch the center of his sleep, but Bisquit, as elusive as ever, slipped out from underneath his outstretched hand. Instead, he walked past Buddy and the other eleven horses and straight to a pile of hay warmed by a few shafts of light coming through the wooden bridge overhead, where he could hear the footsteps of racegoers land heavily on the wood, and fell asleep. This would have enraged a less patient and sleepy man than Buddy to see his prize horse fall asleep with the race less than a half hour away, but he was not angry. For one, he was too tired to do anything to transform even the vaguest impulse into meaningful action, even if that action was to lie down next to Bisquit and fall asleep, and, secondly, he loved this good though never great racehorse too much to ever lay a hand on him.

The other eleven horses stood in awe. "It's a challenge," one of them said.

"A show of dominance," said another.

"A quiet affront to our abilities," said a third.

They felt comfortable speaking in this way because Buddy had left the stables, called up to the stands to break up a fight. Not to be outdone, the other eleven horses also went to sleep, some of them standing, a few of them with their legs tucked under them, and one or two leaning against the stable walls. And because they slept so lightly, disturbed by the noise of the stadium and the knowledge that the race was only minutes away, they dreamed, each horse according to his own mental objects, but each a dream of remarkable similitude.

Bisquit dreamed of the forest where the farmer's wife stood awake and vigilant so long ago. Bisquit stood next to her, and together they watched the traveling salesman hold the farmer's hand in the gold, urging him to take as much as he wanted, and not letting go even when the farmer pulled away. Bisquit watched this little scene, the two men unmoved, until the sun set and he could no longer see them through the dark foliage of the trees. In the morning, the farmer's wife was gone, the farmer too, but the traveling salesman was sitting on a rock next to Bisquit. He said he killed the farmer and his wife while Bisquit was asleep, so now he had plenty of money and a horse, too.

"And with money in the pocket one is at home anywhere," the salesman said, which had never occurred to Bisquit before but seemed quite reasonable. The salesman was as good as any other, and Bisquit rose to meet his new owner. Then he woke up.

The other eleven horses had dreams of their own, similar to each other's, but unlike human dreams. Humans dream of flying or running in open fields, performing feats of physical grace, but horses do not because those things are commonplace to them. Horses dream of money. They are as enchanted by it, the possibility of counting out a row of bills or setting a stack of coins down on a table, as we are enchanted by magical forests or falling through space. They desire our freedoms just as we desire theirs, and yet ours are as unremarkable to us as theirs are to them.

But that is neither here nor there. For now, the race was on. The other eleven horses awoke and joined Bisquit, who was already waiting in the tunnel flanked on both sides by a pair of trumpeters. Councilwoman Venutti climbed to the top of the platform, surrounded by the mayor and all of the important political figures in the town. They all despised horseracing but came to the first race of the year, to show their support, as long as they did not have to mix with the crowd and remained invisible from view, thanks to a large crimson panel that divided them from the people, a panel which Buddy looked at with great admiration, having designed, constructed, and assembled it in a single hour.

Councilwoman Venutti heaved her big red body to the top of the platform and rang the bell till it broke with a twang. The horses entered leisurely, directed one by one into their stalls by two blonde children with tiny whips.

Bisquit stood in his stall waiting for the gun. A jockey came and mounted him. He had almost forgotten about that part. It didn't matter. Now the race was happening, and he had prepared for it as best as he could, but felt nervous all the same, and calmed himself with a story while he waited for the gun:

Once a farmer bought himself a pony for his birthday. For the pony's birthday, that is. How did the farmer know it was the pony's birthday? Because when he went to the horse market that pony had a little birthday cake in front of its stable. Someone had put it there, someone who knew better. The farmer paid for the pony in cash and took him home, and when the farmer's wife saw him she threw her arms around the pony's neck and kissed him and gave him a name: Bisquit.

Bisquit liked his new home; his stable was small but clean, and the farmer owned a small field of clover where Bisquit could roam. This was agreeable to Bisquit, who liked his stable clean and his clover fresh. Every day the farm boy would come and feed Bisquit and every night the farmer's wife would come and brush his mane and kiss him on the snout. Bisquit was happy in his new home and everyone was happy with Bisquit.

He had a little kingdom, though of modest means, and the best company he could hope for, while it lasted.

It did not last. That summer was especially dry, though not so dry that the famer concerned himself too much about it, and was followed by a fall where no rain fell and a snowless winter and a spring where rain fell everywhere but there, so that, by the beginning of the following summer, the farmer and his wife had to abandon the farm for the city.

By this time, they were all rail thin, and Bisquit's mane had grown thin and brittle. But the farmer and his wife loved Bisquit so much that they could not bring themselves to kill him, though their stomachs asked them to go against their hearts at least twenty times a day.

On the road to the city they met a traveling salesman who had plenty of money but no horse. He offered to buy Bisquit on the spot for a decent sum, enough to put the farmer and his wife up at a lodge for the season until the drought ended and they could return to the farm.

"Yes, yes, that's a fair price," the farmer said and reached into the salesman's bag, which was full of gold, and the salesman held his hand there, even when the farmer tried to pull away, and said he could take as much as he wanted. But the farmer's wife saw the deception in this and ran into the forest with Bisquit, where they hid until the traveling salesman grew impatient and went on his way.

In the city, people were prosperous and unfriendly; to the farmer's surprise, they were unaffected by the lack of rain. They could always truck fish in from the sea or grains from more abundant farms on the other side of the mountains. The people lived lavishly; they stayed up late and slept in during the day and were attended by an army of servants who worked around the clock and were paid very little. The farmer and his wife found work as servants in a large house owned by a banker and his son. Bisquit was allowed to live in one of the empty closets next to the garage, and although he never saw the sun and was only given one small meal a day of dry oats, he remained hopeful and sustained his optimism with pleasant memories of the farm, his romps in the clover, and his clean, bright stable, and the farmer's wife who would lovingly brush his mane each night. The farmer's wife still came each night to brush his mane, but now she was tired and distracted, her hands shook from lack of food, and she only had the energy to take him one time around the banker's gravel lot before stuffing him back in the closet and saying goodnight without a kiss.

This went on for many months. The farmer and his wife toiled away in the banker's house, scrubbing floors and washing windows, cooking all the meals, maintaining the grounds, and having to work twice as long as the other servants, who already worked long hours, in order to pay for Bisquit's room and board.

One day, the farmer's wife was in the long room killing flies with a broom. A few fat and shiny black flies gathered on the windowsill and around the glass, bumping into it again and again, in the hope that this time would be different, and the glass would disappear. The farmer's wife attacked them with the broad end of a broom, but she kept missing, and the flies would scatter but always return, untroubled by her presence. She was so tired and distracted, and her hands shook so much, and she was so suddenly angry, even as she became more and more tired and more and more distracted but then suddenly angry again at the injustice of her condition or of Bisquit's. She identified so closely with the pony, who was actually a horse, a horse of small stature, like herself, no longer growing but forever short, and possibly even shrinking. She could no longer tell the difference between herself and Bisquit, and she thought of her beloved horse locked up in a closet, faring no better than he had at the farm, and it all seemed so unjust, the arbitrary hand that directed Bisquit's fate and hers. Whoever had brought them together in happiness had now separated them in misery. The flies gathered in the windowsill, more numerous than before, fatter and shinier than before, and as the farmer's wife continued to think in this way, she became more physically animated, almost possessed, and pounded the broom harder and harder against the window until she smashed one windowpane and then them all, and the glass glittered all around her feet, and the flies exited through the open window.

The banker's son came running around the corner and into the long room, saying, "What have you done, you crazy woman?"

The farmer's wife didn't know—that is, she couldn't say, but let the broom fall from her hand and began to cry.

"Oh stop with your woman's rhetoric," the banker's son said. "Get out of here before my father comes home and it's twice as bad for you." One of the flies was still hanging around and landed on his shoulder, as if an advisor in the matter. The farmer's wife recovered herself and pleaded her case with the banker's son, which was hopeless, as she knew, but luckily he liked horses and agreed to keep Bisquit. The farmer and his wife were thrown out into the wide world to fend for themselves. They worked for a couple of weeks in a warehouse on the outskirts of town and eventually moved back to the farm, preferring the cruel vicissitudes of nature to the diminishing returns of city life.

Bisquit liked the story. It was difficult to know for certain what followed what or the outcome of any action, whether it would be received with indifference or adulation or set off a series of ever more unpredictable events, and Bisquit felt the terror of that but also the excitement. The jockey set a little red cap on Bisquit's head and attached it to his ears with a complicated arrangement of bobby pins. It was annoying to Bisquit, but he knew there must be a reason for it. Then the gun went off.

Bisquit shot out to an early start, spurred to action by the jockey's heel in his gut. He resented it and felt it unnecessary, but the fear of defeat overcame his disgust, and he went on as the jockey continued kicking and the crowd screamed all around him. The other eleven horses were gaining on him: Roxie and Diamond right at his heels; Johnny, Tommy, and Helterskelter in a dead heat for fourth; and the rest of the pack not far off, with the exception of Buck, who had broken all four legs right out of the gate and was being carried off on a stretcher to the boos and jeers of the fans.

At the end of the first lap, Bisquit was in first, which came as a great surprise to his jockey, who had complained bitterly to anyone who would listen about being assigned to such a pathetic horse. But now he was pleasantly surprised as they rounded the bend and a split time of one minute thirty-six seconds flashed on the screen, which was really not too bad, if you consult the record. The jockey attributed this success to his skillful riding instead of an inspired horse and redoubled his efforts, kicking Bisquit twice as hard in the ribs to the point of drawing blood. Bisquit ran on, and as he ran he continued his story, which had begun to interest him, and that interest kept him going:

The banker's son took an immediate liking to Bisquit. Instead of having him shot publicly as a lesson to the other servants as he initially intended, he had the west wing destroyed, razed the tennis courts, and replaced it all with a pretty red barn and a field perfectly suited to Bisquit's needs. Bisquit couldn't have been happier. The life of a farmer's pony had been tolerable with the steady hand of the farmer and his work, but when that was lost, all was lost. He now much preferred the muted affections and extravagant material displays of the banker's son. Bisquit could romp all day without even leaving his barn and kick up his hooves without any fear of knocking in a wall; he could prance and twirl to his heart's delight and eat seventy different kinds of grasses and clovers without ever having to ration a single blade or leaf of it.

Bisquit was happy again, and happiness, he knew, was not guaranteed in this world. There were times, no doubt, when he thought about the farmer's wife and grew sullen and would wallow for a day or two in the dark side of the barn, but soon enough he would be up and frolicking again, letting his long and lush mane fly in the open field. There were no more excuses not to be happy, and if he wasn't happy with all this, then it was his own fault and no one else's.

The banker's son sat in a window on the second floor, admiring his work and admiring Bisquit, and he would sometimes yell a few words from his window, some incoherent words, because he was drunk or mentally incapacitated. He would wag his tongue and drool and point his finger at Bisquit, then stick it in his mouth, as if to convey some spiritual necessity. Bisquit rose at once and trotted over to his master. That's what Bisquit called him in his head; he called him master, though he had never referred to the farmer or farmer's wife in that way. He trotted to the open window and gave a neigh to his master. The master returned with a wide-mouthed yawn and a little bit of drool and a pointed finger. Bisquit took these messages to heart, though he had to interpret them according to his own rudimentary worldview. He took the master to mean that Bisquit had been saved, but that salvation, being a temporary condition, was subject to the sways of power invested in people like himself (meaning the banker and his son), and though they did not request or deserve it, being subject to the very same eccentricities of fate, they nevertheless must be respected, despite all outward shows of stupidity and ignorance, even unvarnished cruelty and inhumanity, that, through their very limited human means, they still remained conduits for the good and the righteous. This all seemed so true and well said to Bisquit that he returned to his barn and slept easy that night, easier than most, though not without waking once or twice in a blind panic.

Sometimes Bisquit trod lightly over the ground, unsure as to whether it would hold him up or let him fall forever, and at other times he gathered his courage and ran at full speed across the field, not caring whether he went too far and broke through a wall or another dimension. Children came from all over, some from the country and some from the city, to look at Bisquit in his field and feed him at the gate.

The children were a great comfort to Bisquit, and as long as they came to his gate and fed him apple slices and cubes of sugar, all would be right in the world. It was during this time that the banker's son appeared less and less at his window, but Bisquit didn't notice at first, because he was so preoccupied with the children, their soft and moony faces. Even when they were not there, he comforted himself with their presence, though this had become problematic, because at some point he had so built them up in his mind, the image in his mind, that the ideal had surpassed the reality, and the live children began to disappoint even as Bisquit clung to their images, more and more.

It was this disappointment that drove him back to his master's window, but the master was not there. Master almost never appeared at his window anymore, and Bisquit grew anxious. He caught glimpses of him as he passed through the corridors of the house or ran out to meet a guest or leave for the day in his car, but he never came to his window, which was the one place that he would deliver his special messages to Bisquit. This negligence, Bisquit noticed, extended to his fields and barn as well; no one ever came to maintain it. The barn fell into disrepair, the once lustrous red faded to a dull brown, and Bisquit stood inside feeling alone and unloved. The children, as bright and cheerful as ever, came to Bisquit's gate, but he was no longer there to receive them and hardly stirred from his bed of dirty hay, even when they called his name and promised treats and petting. This only increased Bisquit's agony. He knew how much they loved and looked forward to, even depended upon, these daily visits to sustain their belief in a just world, and by not receiving them and locking himself up in the faded red barn that was crumbling all around him, he was not only increasing his own misery but increasing the misery of the whole living lot, and this was a burden to him.

For three days and three nights, Bisquit remained in this state, alternating between numbness and suicidal despair, hindered only by the fact that a horse cannot tie a knot or shoot a gun. This struck Bisquit as so funny, in the grimmest possible way, that it actually cheered him up a little. He moved his head and shook the dirt out of his mane. He felt inspired enough to eat a little bit of dry oats and drink some stale water. Then he rose and moved around in his barn, exercising his stiff legs. His heart shifted, and life seemed better, the master kind and the children sweet and true. He crashed through the doors of the barn, which exploded behind him in a magnificent display of his new resolution, and ran straight to his master's window, where he sent up into the heavens the loudest and most resolute neigh he could muster.

The master came to the window in his pajamas, though it was the middle of the day, and coughed a few times, unable to tolerate the sting of the air on this clear winter day.

The master was sick. His hair was falling out, his skin was pasty and white, and he had lost so much weight that his pajamas were hanging on his fragile and decimated frame. Bisquit felt like a terrible waste of a horse and nearly fell back into his former state before recovering himself and remembering why he had come.

Why had he come? He could not remember. But here he was, and there was the master, and possibly that was enough.

"It's not enough," the master said and coughed a few times to emphasize his point. "And I see you've destroyed the barn, and eaten all seventy kinds of grasses and clovers in the field."

The sky, which had been clear only a few moments ago, clouded over. A few flakes of snow fell from the sky.

"It's never enough for you," the master continued, "because I give and give and give and you just take, take, take. It will never be enough for you, Bisquit, and yet I've given you everything."

The snow fell harder now. Master left his window for a moment but returned with a scarf around his neck and gloves on his hands.

"We're sending you to the racetrack, Bisquit. I have a buddy who wants to buy you and thinks you would make a good though never great racehorse, and I need the money so I can repair the barn and pay off my creditors."

Bisquit couldn't hear anything. The snow was falling so hard now that he almost couldn't see his master. And yet he completely understood. The master was sending him away, and this was the very best thing for both of them.

The master was arranging a few unseen objects on a table and continued talking while he did this, but he was wheezing and coughing so much that Bisquit couldn't make out the words. He motioned with his snout to a rag hanging from a nail on the inside of the window, probably used to wipe the windowsill, and the master took the rag and gave his nose a good blow. He soaked the rag through with blood, and the red stood out sharply as the snow fell all around them, now coming up to Bisquit's knees. Then he took the rag and threw it at Bisquit, but it missed and landed a few feet away from him. Bisquit watched the red rag bleed into the surrounding snow. He moved toward it so that his master would not feel embarrassed at what poor aim he had.

The master returned to the unseen objects on his table, which, though probably a trifle for the master, something to distract him from his troubles, some game or puzzle or doll shaped in the likeness of himself, took on the greatest importance for Bisquit, who strained his eyes to see them through the driving snow. The master continued talking, and Bisquit listened without hearing or needing to hear the exact words; and as the master spoke at length and in great detail of his troubles, Bisquit remained strangely agreeable, bowing his head in acknowledgment of his master's words.

The snow was falling so hard now that the bloody rag was buried. Bisquit stood still, up to his neck in snow, straining to see his master once more. And even when the children broke free from the gate, dressed in coats and hats, singing carols and pulling sleds, and even when they threw every kind of rope and pulley over Bisquit's back to haul him out of the snow and onto the road where a truck was waiting to take him to the racetrack, even then Bisquit did not break away from his master, still fiddling with his assemblage of invisible objects on the table. Bisquit never looked away, not once; it was master who looked away, who broke away.

Back in the race, Bisquit grew tired not physically, for he could have run all day and twice as fast if he wanted to, but in his heart he grew weary, although at the same time fearful of defeat, and it was fear that kept him going through the second leg of the race, that and shame, for he was a proud horse, or had at least learned what pride meant; and though he cared nothing for winning horse races and would rather be in the forest with the farmer's wife or under his master's window or even sleeping next to Buddy under the oak tree, still he couldn't stand the idea of letting someone down, whoever that person might be.

These were his thoughts as he finished the second lap, now even with six of the horses; he could see their snouts on all sides, bobbing up and down, like a family of porpoises coming up for air, and the multicolored jockeys on their backs, who were sure to take the glory though they did none of the work, and at this thought a wave of indifference rose in Bisquit's heart as he slackened his pace just slightly, but without losing much ground, for the other horses must have felt the same way.

Two more laps to go, or possibly three; he actually didn't know. Buddy never discussed the technical aspects of the race with him, afraid that it might interfere with his pure pursuit of victory, and so Bisquit ran on, unsure of when the race would end or what its purpose might be.

He was trailing all the horses but two. Big Dog and Trixie had injured themselves, bravely finishing the race but without any chance of winning it, while Bisquit ran on, picking off Roxie and Diamond, who were sucking the air, then Johnny and Tommy, whose apathy overcame them in the end, and finally Raymond, Princess, and Little Dog, who ran even and together created a drag on themselves, given the aerodynamic oddities of the stadium. This left Bisquit and Helterskelter in a tie for first.

Helterskelter was an especially tenacious competitor not because of his extremes but because of his plateaus. He always ran at the same pace and always won, though he cared as much about winning as he did about losing, and you could put him on the winner's podium or in a trash heap and it was all the same to him. Buddy had given him his name in the hopes of lighting a fire in his belly, but it was contrary to his nature, which was even and temperate to the end. He moved forward as if on a conveyor belt with a stone jockey on his back, taking in the light of eternity. Bisquit ran beside him, laboring the whole way, as they entered the fourth and final lap.

And now the crowd was on its feet, screaming and jumping up and down, one at a time, each in his own time, but nevertheless coordinated in a tremendous show of solidarity. They screamed his name and hoisted their children onto their shoulders and threw their arms around one another, friends and strangers alike. Granted, the people were so drunk that not one of them would be able to drive home or even walk ten feet without the assistance of a more sober friend, yet the alcohol allowed them to scream what they could never say sober, that their hearts were filled with love without an object, and that condition was a painful one indeed, but now they had found one to receive their dammed affections and that one was Bisquit.

Bisquit heaved himself forward with each step, determined to win. He fell defeated, and yet the moment he hit the ground, defeat propelled him closer to victory. None of his limbs obeyed him, his tail hung limp as if he were at rest in his barn, while his frizzy mane flew all around him, magnetized by the air, which felt cooler now, and drier, and full of the electricity of fall. The aspen leaves crowning the stadium turned yellow and transparent and broke free from the trees, covering every surface of the stadium with a waxy gold. Bisquit ran on, leading Helterskelter by a foot now, a small lady's foot. Two Monarch butterflies landed on his eyes, but he shook them away, so they flew to Helterskelter, whose jockey reached out and pinned them to his vest.

Bisquit was winning, and yet, his jockey had already dismounted, had lost interest, and was chatting with a couple of farm girls in the stands. Buddy helped Councilwoman Venutti descend from the political platform. She thanked him and went on her way. The crimson panel fell with a thud, the stadium filled up with trash, the revelers made for the exits, a little more sober now and resigned to their lives outside the racetrack, for though they loved Bisquit, they had bet on other horses, horses with a reputation for victory and not mere potential and idealism. Still, the race went on, even as the stadium emptied, and Bisquit was alone, for Helterskelter too had given up not because he was losing but because no one was watching, and now Bisquit continued to dominate the race, even as he lost all of his competitors and all of his fans. No one saw Bisquit and no one ever had, and he wondered as he came to a stop a few inches before the finish line what might be terrible in that and what might be liberating.

"Bravo!" said a voice. The stadium was empty, and that emptiness reminded Bisquit of the averted eyes of his master, and he assumed the voice was his.

It was the master. He had returned. Bisquit stepped back from the finish line and toward the tunnel, where the voice emanated.

"Master's dead," the voice said, "as you very well know," and this stung Bisquit, who did not like being spoken to like a child. And though the master wasn't there, Bisquit's body didn't know the difference and reacted with the same mixture of love, hatred, and fear that the master had imprinted upon him.

The man stepped out of the tunnel, but Bisquit didn't recognize him. He was taller than Master, with long fingers and a long neck and hair combed slick across his forehead.

Bisquit did not want to engage with this man but could not leave except through the tunnel, and the man was blocking the path. He pretended to look at a few red and orange leaves gathered in a corner of the track, as if they were of the greatest interest to him, but the man remained, looking at Bisquit and waiting for him to come closer. Finally Bisquit did, because the sun was going down, and the air was so cold now, and he tried to do it quickly, but the man was fast and held him by the reins and put his face in Bisquit's face and said:

"I want to buy you Bisquit."

This was a strange proposition to Bisquit, who had always gone willingly to wherever he was wanted and never needed to be bribed or bought.

Now Bisquit recognized him not from memory, because his life had made that impossible, but from fantasy. It was the traveling salesman. Bisquit did not recognize his face but his bag, the same bag he had carried with him that day on the road.

"Listen, Bisquit," he said, "I'm not a cruel man, but my life has been hard, and I've come all this way, and I won't be denied again."

Bisquit nodded, keeping one eye on the tunnel, should the salesman loosen his grip and give him a chance to escape. The man continued talking but held a firm grip on the reins:

"I left home early and went south seeking my fortune, peddling anything I could to anyone who would buy it, selling the faultiest products to the most destitute of people. From the time I was a boy, I had a knack for it, and though my parents didn't love me, they gave me a sturdy mind and a quick wit, and for that I am thankful."

Bisquit didn't know where this was going. He didn't find the traveling salesman to be witty at all, and he had had a long day and wanted to go home.

"Sure, I cheated everyone I came across and was always sure to leave town at the exact right time, at the breaking point, I called it, because if you do what I do for as long as I have done it, you know there's a point, at which everything turns, everyone wakes up and realizes they have been duped. This always happens all at once, never individually but collectively—and no one decides it in advance or even discusses it, but suddenly they are at your door and screaming for your head. It was like that, again and again for me I couldn't tell you how many times, Bisquit, before the first rap at the front door I was at the back, making my escape. And in this way I grew rich but with very little company, because I trusted no one enough to let them near me."

Bisquit felt sorry for this man and at the same time admired his daring, though it was born of desperation and therefore didn't count. The master at least retained his dignity, not running from town to town like some craven rat but growing his empire through ever more subtle means and emissaries unseen, so that he could always be at his window, where he was needed by Bisquit. And that was the difference, Bisquit thought, between the master and the traveling salesman. The master always appeared at his window; anyone could see him there, or could until the end, when it was his time to go, to submit to the whims of an all-powerful structure that he himself had created or his father created and he merely maintained. And all this was so different than the traveling salesman, who waited in the darkness of the tunnel to spring himself on an unsuspecting horse, to distract him from winning his first horse race, and to make an offer on the spot to buy him when he was too tired and weak to say no, though he wanted more than anything to go home and go to sleep.

"I cheated everyone," the traveling salesman continued, "and returned to the north a rich man, with a bag full of gold and everything I could want" Here he broke off and looked at the ground, and, moved by his own story, his body slackened enough to drop Bisquit's reins, but Bisquit stayed for a moment, because he felt bad for the man and wanted to hear the end of the story.

"I had everything but a horse," the man said, "and when I saw you on the road with that pathetic farmer and his wife making their way to the city, where they would surely perish, I thought I had myself a horse and even offered them more than you were worth not because I felt sorry for them, because we all get what we deserve in this life, but because I wanted to throw my weight around, show them how much I had, and how much I could spare."

Bisquit nodded. The story was a familiar one, though it meant nothing to him.

"Imagine my humiliation Bisquit, my anger and humiliation, to be denied by a couple of country clowns!"

Bisquit looked at the traveling salesman, still holding his bag of gold, the same that he had carried that day, and almost laughed but didn't because horses can't laugh. It was strange to hear how, even as precarious as Bisquit's life had been and subject to a fate he did not understand, as powerless as he was and always had been, he still exerted a certain amount of power over this man, though he had directed his fate without any kind of intentionality and derived no pleasure from it. Though actually, at the moment, it brought him a certain amount of pleasure, and he tried to conceal this, because he did not want to appear cruel.

"And when I held the farmer's hand in the gold, I thought for certain the horse would be mine, even as he drew his hand away, and I held it there, but the deceitful farmer's wife ran into the forest, and I couldn't find her or you and grew impatient and went on my way."

Bisquit thought the story was becoming repetitive and that the traveling salesman was now torturing himself with the pain of his memories, but he continued talking:

"After that day I looked everywhere for another horse, but everywhere I looked I was disappointed and resolved to find you, though I had no idea where to begin. I went to the city and bribed every housekeeper and innkeeper, but no one had seen you. They took my money but filled my ears with lies. I was about to give up, to leave town, when I saw the children at the gate and knew by the way that they talked in their childish ways about a horse at the banker's house that it must be you because children in their innocence have not learned to deceive anyone or have not been put in a position where they must deceive. I went to the banker's house to inquire about you and was turned away many times. He loved to torture me by saying no again and again or saying yes but then breaking off negotiations suddenly or raising the price at the last minute, to take his offer off the table and out of my reach. I sent him a final offer that day at the window—everything I had—and even then he was toying with me. And then when he went and sold you to the racetrack for almost nothing, I felt the true depth of his cruelty and went straight to his house to kill or at least maim him but could not because he was already dead."

Bisquit was becoming tired of the traveling salesman, but was afraid to leave at this critical moment, when he had worked himself into such a state that he might lash out at him and later regret it.

"I followed you to the racetrack. That part was easy because there's only one in town, but Mr. Buddy kept such a vigilant watch over you that I could never get near you. I was biding my time, crouched in the hills with my bag of gold, waiting for the perfect time to make an offer."

The traveling salesman smiled, and a little piece of greasy hair fell into his eyes, and this sickened Bisquit, who could see what a sad and desperate man he was and probably always had been. He would walk with him as far as the shed, and then he would let him down easy and send him on his way. He had no use for his money. Though it enchanted him, he knew that enchantment would evaporate the moment he had it and preferred to keep it at a distance, where it would retain its magic.

Together they walked through the tunnel and into the dark night, a starless night, but with a moon that hung full in the sky, lending a white lining to the house and the hills and the leafless trees. They walked past Buddy's house, and Bisquit looked inside the window and saw him asleep in his bed. He tried to make as much noise as possible, going out of his way to walk through piles of dry leaves and snap twigs with his hooves, but Buddy did not stir. And now Bisquit resigned himself to the life of a crooked salesman's horse, just as he had before to the life of a lowly farmer's horse or the house pet of a banker's son or a good though never great racehorse. They made it as far as the oak tree, where the traveling salesman tried to mount him, but awkwardly, because he had never been on a horse before. Bisquit looked up into the branches of the oak tree and beneath, where he had spent so many happy days, and all around the field, where Buddy had trained him to be a racehorse. That's funny, Bisquit thought, I didn't notice all these young saplings where grass used to grow, and he admired the industry of Buddy so much, who even as he was preparing the stadium for the race and training the racehorses, made time to plant new trees in the field, which would soon be a splendid orchard, given the number and variety of the saplings. They were planted everywhere—there must have been thousands—and they began to move in the soft wind of this fall night. And yet they were moving in a way that trees do not move, which is to say they were walking and carrying weapons of all kinds as they approached Bisquit and called out to the traveling salesmen and named his crimes. Buddy was among them and the farmer and his wife, the children at the gate, and all of the people who had been cheated over the years. The traveling salesman yelled for mercy, but they knocked the bag of gold out of his hands and threw a rope over one of the branches, where they strung him up in a hurry; they didn't even bother to get a chair but stood the traveling salesman on Bisquit's back and kicked Bisquit out from under him and watched the salesman swing to his death.

Bisquit lay for a few minutes on his side and waited for the mob to disperse. Buddy came and threw a red blanket over him and told him it wasn't his fault, but it had to be done, for horse-stealing was a crime punishable by death in these parts. Bisquit knew that was a lie, or at least a partial lie, because the traveling salesmen had tried to buy him three times and had three times been denied. Then Buddy said: "You're free to go, Bisquit, because you've fulfilled your service, but you're also welcome to stay, and we'd love to have you."

Then Buddy kissed Bisquit on the forehead and said goodnight. Bisquit could hear a few people take the traveling salesman's body down from the tree and the clank of instruments as they buried him. Eventually the children came over and petted him, but half-heartedly, because they were tired and unaccustomed to staying up so late. The farmer and his wife came over, too, and stood him up and gave him an apple to eat. In the morning, Buddy looked out his window, over the mound of earth where the man was buried, and the oak tree and the fields beyond, to the place where Bisquit had been. Now he was gone, but where he had gone no one knew.

Acknowledgments

I WANT TO THANK MY FATHER for hiding in the bathroom and reading sci-fi novels when I was growing up. You taught me what books were for: relieving constipation and getting away from your family. I want to thank my mother, too, for sending me to Catholic school and instilling in me a love of musicals, helping to shape the fun-loving and doom-laden artistic sensibility that you'll find in these pages. Thank you to all of my teachers: the nuns at Holy Angels, Judy Bunch and Mr. Bruns, Leonard Schwartz, Bill Ransom, Ernestine Kimbro, and Mary Anne Bright. Thank you to the editors at *Fairy Tale Review*, *Black Scat Review*, *The Champagne Room*, *Unbroken*, *Juked*, *Western Humanities Review*, *Mid-American Review*, *Gobshite Quarterly*, and *Modern Grimmoire: Contemporary Fairy Tales, Fables, and Folklore* who previously published stories from this book. Thanks to Sara and your copy of *Black Beauty*, which is the obvious literary predecessor for Bisquit. Thanks to support from the University of Massachusetts, the University of Denver, and the Evan Frankel Foundation. Thanks to Graham Foust for reading the book carefully, to Brian Kiteley for sponsoring it, and to the FC2 editorial board for publishing it. Most of all, I want to thank Carl. Without you I would never have persevered through all the bullshit.